Moricka Burgess published her works, *"Shadows"* in the International Library of Poetry and the Long Island Chronicle. She was also a freelance writer for Adelphi University and Howard "The Hilltop" University, on topics ranging from ethnic and social issues to plays and theatrical performances. Throughout her life, she has worked on more than a dozen projects as a writer and actor in New York for religious institutions and colleges. She co-authored the influential collection of poems *"Seasons, the Turn of Life"* in 2005 and its reprint *"Seasons, beautifully, Me"* in 2020. She has a collection of short stories and is completing a second book as part of a series to her current book, Don't Call Me Love.

Moricka pulls her stories from her family, community, and work in the labor movement fighting for working people and against injustice- over the past three decades. She currently resides in Vincentown, New Jersey.

MORICKA BURGESS

DON'T CALL ME LOVE

Love Never Fails!

Moricka Burgess

ISBN: 9798377956181

Moricka burgess has always been marvelous. Her drive to better herself pushed her friends and family to do better. Her bright sense of fashion influenced the style choices of the children she raised. Her music and singing filled every corner of her home. Moricka would instill a rule of working hard, but still having fun. She nurtured the creative writing skills of many others including her nephew.

Even when the world belittles her, Moricka burgess is still a marvel. In the darkest times, when she thought no one could see her, she showed strength in her tears. You can't help but feel it when you are near her. Each word spoken with an unwavering confidence that can only be earned. Whether she is wrong or right, her words still project power.

It's a trait not many people have. Sure, some people, like politicians or cops, speak with authority. But that comes from their title, not from the person. Along with nepotism and popularity, mediocrity often turns into authority. For Moricka, nothing is ordinary. She has fought tooth and nail to be the marvel that she is.

IZZY B.

To every dreamer and the loved ones standing beside them. Don't Give Up and for heaven sake, Don't Wake Up! Keep dreaming until your dreams become reality

Acknowledgements

With thanks to Gordon R Burgess, Shirley M Smith for being my parents, the Burgess Family, Dr. Monique L. Rodgers, D.M.,Pauline Mendo, Getwriteoncoaching and WriteOn Publications, the Editors, the Marketing Team

And special thanks to Brian Maxwell

DON'T CALL ME LOVE

1

HE'S NOT COMING

∞**THE DAY I** inwardly die happens to fall on my 17th birthday. To be precise, it was a dull Wednesday. The raindrops outside changed from mini droplets to violent storms, falling from the sky. There was nothing, then everything swallows me up. A group of faceless people who are invading my space usher me down a corridor while they babble. I float down the halls on their words and brace myself for what comes next. A woman breaks me away from the pack and leads me into a notably cold room with three massive windows and white walls. I notice two bloodstained, gory looking people connected by tubes to two loudly beeping machines. The floating words become coherent. She tells me the people lying on the hospital beds are my parents after a horrible car crash.

When I wake, I can't shake the memory of my parent's accident. A fresh memory that won't wash away like the rain no matter how hard I wish it was just a dream. But why think of this now? Suddenly, a hazy white cloud envelops me. Why is it so bright in here? I squint to lessen the sting of its glow. Where am I? I search the surroundings to make out my location. On my right is a half-open curtain, which hides an empty bed. Now, the memories make sense, I'm in a hospital. Only this time, I'm the patient.

"Well hello there, Ms. Dickerson."
I don't notice when the woman standing over me enters the room. I blink twice till she comes into focus.
"There, there." She places a cold clammy hand on my shoulder. "I'm glad to see you have finally woken up. Must've been some kinda dream you were having. You've been out for days." I struggle to read

her lips as my ears play catch up with the sound waves bouncing off her tongue. "My name is Nurse Agnes. And you are at Mountainside Hospital."

"How long did you say I've been here?" I try to swallow, but my mouth and throat feel like dust. I watch her standing perfectly upright in her pale pink scrubs, hair pushed back into a bun, glasses and pudgy waist.

"A few days."

"Excuse me? A few days? Are you sure?"

"Yes. You came in on Monday evening and today is Wednesday."

"Wow it seems like a couple hours ago I was home in bed."

"I can only imagine. Do you remember what happened Ms. Dickerson?"

"No, not really."

"When you arrived you were in pretty bad shape. You lost quite a bit of blood."

"I did?" I sink into the bed and turn my face toward the beeping IV machine. It soothes me and the blinking red light is hypnotic.

"Yes you did, Ms. Dickerson?"

I turn back toward the nurse. "Can you call me Arianna? Whenever you say Ms. Dickerson, I look around for someone older."

"Of course. Do you remember the cuts Arianna? How did they get all over your arms and wrist?"

"Not really." I look down at the bed and smooth out the scratchy beige blankets and crisp white sheets. Above my hands, my arms are thickly bandaged.

"May I send someone in here to speak with you about it?"

"Is it Brian?" My eyes widen as I look up at her.

"Who's Brian?" The nurse squints her eyes. "Is he your husband?"

I shake my head. "No we're not married."

"Do you know how I can find him? Perhaps he can shed some light on what happened?"

I don't say anything. I have a response, but the words will not come out. What I want to say is yes please call him! Tell him I'm here and need to see him. Tell him I apologize.

14

"Ms. Dickerson, I mean Arianna, do you know where I can find Brian?" When she looks at me, I woefully cling to the kindness of her expression.

I was going to give her his cell; I knew it by heart. Instead, I say, "Try the train station. He'll still be there waiting if the freight trains are running off schedule."

"What?"

"Nothing... never mind."

"Would you like to speak with someone while you wait on Brian?"

I roll onto my side which takes a while because my body feels like a cement block. I'm guessing that's because I've been lying in the same position for over two-days.

"No. But can I have a minute? I'm feeling really tired?" I turn back toward the IV machine.

"Certainly." She places her hand on my shoulder and this time it is warm and dry. "I'll be back in a little while. Then we can finish our conversation, okay?" She walks to the door, then, stops. "Are you hungry?"

"No, just tired."

When I hear the old squeaky door close, I roll on my back and stare up at the white ceiling. I'm not a fan of hospitals. They remind me of a great wall in a burial site. Though many enter, not all make it out alive. I guess that's why it feels like a morgue. You'd think with the large windows and bursts of sunlight coming in, or the natural body heat-would lessen the cold. Not true.

I'm glad I'm the only patient in the room. I don't want anyone to see me here. And more importantly, I'm not the cordial type, faking a hint of concern for a neighboring patient and asking questions about their condition or sharing about these bandages on my arms, are not me. I try my best to get comfortably situated, shifting around in the bed, but a stinging pain shoots up my right arm from my wrist when the IV moves and pinches my skin.

Suddenly, the heaviness of the moment coupled by the medication coursing through me weighs me down. I simply want to drift off for a while. *How did I get here?* "You know this is the last place in the world- you ever thought you'd return to, Arianna. You musta' been pretty bad off to end up here- grrl?" I slur my words as sleep creeps up on me.

∞∞∞∞

"Excuse me, do you know what time it is?" I ask the first person I see.

"Nah, I left my watch at home." The finely dressed man smiles politely.

"Thanks anyway."

"No worries."

I hadn't gotten back to my seat when he called.

"Hey miss?"

"Yes."

"It's a quarter to," he points up at the prompter.

"Really? Wow I didn't even see that clock." I chuckle. "I guess the 6:28am train is running late, again- huh?"

"Yeah, it would seem so." He smiles at me, and I quiver. "I'm waiting on that one too. You heading to DC?"

"Yes."

"Well, when it gets here, save me a seat, eh."

The words flow easily off his tongue. His confidence is refreshing, and I'm spooked by how quickly I'm drawn to him. What if he's a serial killer? Still, without hesitation, I reply, "Will do."

Within minutes, I hear the whistling train horn as it thunders toward me. I take one step back from the edge of the platform when the ground shudders beneath my feet and a gust of wind makes me jolt when it stops. People quickly board the train, seem annoyed by its lateness, and eager to be destination bound. I walk up the aisle looking for an empty seat. In the first car I board I see a familiar face. The intriguing man from earlier is sitting by himself. He pulls out a folder full of papers, a laptop and cell phone which he immediately starts punching away at to make a call. While he is fixated on the caller, I quietly plant myself in the empty seat beside him. He thumbs

16

through a stack of papers, marking each page as he addresses the caller.

I sit in silence call after call while he's on the phone with what I hope are all work related. I glance out at the landscapes and old buildings as the fast-paced Acela train whisks by. Or nervously tapping my nails on the mini folding tray table. Surprisingly, the sound of the melody comforts me.

"You heading to DC for work or pleasure?" He finally asks.

"Seriously?" I smirk at him, "Work of course. Why else would I be up this early in the cold, no less, waiting on a train I know is always running late."

"True." He shrugs. "I guess you don't have to ask me that then-huh? But, you know it is not the train's fault it is always running late, though."

"Oh no?" I tilt my head. "Then whose blasted fault is it?"

"Blasted- wow. I haven't heard that B word in years. It's the freight company's blasted fault," he says with a laugh. "Like in Monopoly the train doesn't own the railroad line. It's owned by the freight company so if there's a freight that needs to move down the line—everything else is at a standstill till it's done!"

"Really? I never knew." I lean in toward him, concentrating on his eyes, "Are you telling the truth?"

Without blinking, he crisscrosses his finger over his heart and says, "Scouts honor."

"Were you really a boy scout?"

"For sure, a long time ago. And you say *"really"* a lot"

I smile. "Look at this- I learned something new."

"I know, you see there, that should show you-"

"What?"

"You need me in your life."

"Wow, my entire life, yeah?"

"Yep."

"Well, you *sure* are cocky." I pause. "See, I didn't use *really*."

He smirks. "Nah beautiful, just confident."

"Okay confident, do you have a name?"

"Brian and you?" He reaches for my hand to shake it.

"Ms. Arianna Dickerson." I softly grip his smooth strong hand. "By the way, you should write that down so you can contact me later."

"Now who's the confident one?" He shoots the sexiest smile I've ever seen on men.

"What can I say, in such a short time 'the boy scout' has rubbed off on me?" I send a flirty wink his way.

"Ladies and Gentlemen next stop will be Washington, DC in 18 minutes," the conductor calls over the paging system, "Gather all your belongings. Washington, DC will be the next and final stop."

"Quick, we don't have much time. Tell me a little bit about yourself?"

"Let's see you know my name. What's next?" he pauses. "Oh yeah, I am the youngest of five. I have four older sisters. My Mom and Pop are still together living in Brooklyn. How about you?"

"It's only me. I have a couple of cousins. Tell me something else?" I say gleefully.

"You are an enthusiastic one, aren't you?" He looks surprised, "What'd ya want to know?"

"Try something simple, like what do you do?"

"Let's see, I'm a negotiator."

I sit up. "Ooh like a police negotiator. You talk people into letting hostages go?" I lean in close.

"Nah beautiful, you watch way too much TV." He grins. "I'm a contract negotiator for a union."

"Union contracts that sounds interesting."

"What about you?"

"I sell real estate. I'm an agent."

"Oh like a FBI agent, ah!" He says mockingly.

"No funny man I know you heard me say real estate agent." We both laugh.

While, Brian speaks, I give him a thorough once over, looking more closely than I have since meeting him, almost two-hours ago. He wears his huge smile like a classy outfit. His pearly white teeth fit his mouth perfectly. Few men can pull off a big smile without looking clownish. He seems about 5' 11 or 6ft. His green eyes flatter his light smooth clear sesame skin, and I notice his eyes change in color when

18

the sun kisses them. But those bow legs when he walks "hallelujah" it's enough to make me swoon. Yum! Our conversation flows easily.

"Now for something a little deeper," I grab his hand.

"Oh no we're doing this already?" He huffs, then smiles.

"It'll be harmless," I smile back at him. "Tell me something no one else knows. Tell me a secret."

"A secret huh. Whoa, you know how to go for the jugular. You know we just met, right?"

"What, you don't trust me?" I bat my lashes profusely.

He smiles. "Trust, that's a big T word for a first encounter. But, somehow you seem strangely familiar to me."

"I know, right. Now, stop procrastinating."

"Okay, here goes nothing." He slides up in the booth about ten inches from my face. "Every day," he pauses. "Without fail I call my Mom. She's my ace. She knows everything about me"

"What do you talk about?"

"Everything. Mostly I call to check in on her."

"Aw, that's so sweet. I wasn't expecting that. And-" I crisscross my finger over my heart, "your secret's safe with me. I'm sitting next to a real life Mama's boy."

"Oh that's how it is huh?" He loosens his grip and leans back into his booth.

"No... no... no," I grab his hands and pull him toward me, "I'm only kidding. Family is everything. And a man who loves his mother, I figure will do no less for me."

"Cool so now it's your turn. Tell me some-"

I interrupted him. "Why? You are much more interesting. I have a ton of follow up questions."

"That's not how this works. Getting to know someone goes both ways." He says pointing at us.

"I don't have any secrets. I'm an open book."

"Then there's a lot to tell. I haven't read you yet."

I squirm in my seat, uneasy. "Let me think for a minute. I'm used to asking the questions. That's so much easier."

"Washington, DC- last and final stop, Washington, DC. Please watch your step when you exit the train. There is a gap between the train and the platform," the conductor walks down the aisle calling.

Brian grabs his laptop, collects his papers drafted on the stylish canary linen paper that I gather are union contracts and two-binders from off the tabletop. He stands up to put on his coat, then looks at me. "You coming? We haven't finished telling our secrets, have we?" He asks.

My smile is answer enough for him.

2

PAGING ARIANNA

∞**I MUST'VE LET** myself drift again. Bright lights, loud noises as the translucent mixture enters through my veins. Drip. Drip. But I can feel the breeze of the sleek silver train pushing against me as it sweeps by me in a blur while I'm back on the station platform. I linger in a place between my dream and the horrible reality. The best thing would be for me to remain adrift.

"Ms. Dickerson?"

I jump at the sight of Nurse Agnes hovering over me, I place my IV-free hand on my chest. "Whoa you're like a ninja nurse. It's Arianna, remember?"

"I didn't mean to wake you." She pauses, snaps her finger and nods her head. "Right, sorry, calling people by their last name is a force of habit. I'll get it right. Arianna, did you reconsider what I asked you the other day?"

"Uh- Umm." I give her a puzzled look.

"I asked you if you would be interested in speaking with someone."

"Oh right, who is it?"

"Dr. Staten."

"A psychiatrist?"

"Well you can meet her and ask her who she is." Her smile changes to a more serious gaze. This one is an air of concern.

"She's a psychiatrist." I say it with a huff.

"It can't hurt Arianna." Her smile widens when she remembers to call me by my first name.

"Ah you got it," I say, encouraging her.

"Especially since it seems you were looking for someone to talk to. Speak to her and if you don't like it- don't ask her to return."

"Can I ask you a question? All jokes aside-"

"Yes." She steps toward me.

"Why do you think I need to speak with someone?"

She purses her lips a moment to think. "You just look like you can use someone to listen to you."

"Ok, whatever- send her by."

"Great, she's outside!"

"Whoa, I guess I really look crazy to you because you didn't waste any... time," I say playfully. Agnes simply smiles and walks out.

I'm not sure what meeting with this psych lady will do but I'm ready for some live entertainment and the extra body heat. "What's the worst that can happen? If I don't like her- then she's outta here!" I say it aloud.

"Ms. Dickerson, hi my name is Dr. Amanda Staten." This psyche lady is prettier than I imagine. Though, she wears a white unflattering doctor's coat. But the way it falls against her body, I can tell she works out. Her medium brown skin seems ageless. Not, one, mark, or blemish on her face. She has a nice smile and kind brown eyes, similar to Nurse Agnes. Yes, she certainly understands love.

"Hi. It's Arianna. I'm getting sick and tired of everyone calling me Ms. Dickerson," I snap.

"Well then Arianna," she nods up and down slowly with each word, "I wanted to come by to introduce myself and chat briefly," when she pauses the nodding stops. "Then if you'd like we can set another time for a longer conversation. If that's ok with you?"

"Yes but I'm not going to be here much longer," I'm not certain what I'm saying is the truth, instead more like wishful thinking.

"Not a problem. If after being discharged, you would like to continue talking, we can always schedule something later. I have an office outside of the hospital."

"Good." I grumble. "I'm so not a fan of hospitals."

"Oh why is that?" She asks it like she wants to know.

"I just don't like them," I snapped again, this time not meaning to.

"Didn't you bring yourself here?" Dr. Staten's tone remains calm, despite how often I snap at her.

"I'm not sure."

"Ok- a minor lapse in time is understandable."

"Is it?"

"Yes, it is." She pauses. "Let's try this another way. How's it going so far?"

"I'm trying to remember what happened that got me all bandaged up like this."

"Oh, then you do remember walking into the emergency room, right?"

"Yes I remember walking into the ER. I'm just trying to replay the moments before coming here." My harsh tone doesn't give her much to work with.

"Then maybe I can help jog your memory?" She smiles. "But before we go back to replaying the past few days let's talk a little bit about how you're feeling. Are you in any pain?"

"You know you look familiar to me. Have we met before?" I ask.

"I don't know. Perhaps, I just have one of those faces. Now, back-"

"No seriously, where's your office?"

"It's in Woodbridge off of Rahway Avenue."

"Near the Rahway Prison?"

"Yes, about a mile and a half down the road. Do you visit that prison often?"

"No," I say laughing. I bet she thinks I'm a psychotic ex-criminal. "My church is near there. Have you heard of Dominion Church?"

Dr. Staten nods. "Ah yes, I hold group sessions there on Friday evenings. Pastor Jacobs cares for the soul, body and especially the mind. How about I leave some information about the group sessions at the nurses station to put in your chart, so you'll have it when you're discharged? Would you like to try a session with at least one other person?"

"Oh." I lean back in the bed and turn away from her.

"Arianna," she raises her voice slightly, "like I said earlier let's take this slow and know anything we discuss is confidential. I can't share a report with anyone."

"That's good." I ease up in the bed, turn to face her again and smile.

"Now Arianna, are you in any pain?"

"All the time," I say the first honest thing I have said to anyone in weeks.

∞∞∞∞

I HOP ON the Garden State Parkway heading south in my black velvet on cappuccino leather interior Lincoln MKZ, leaving Mountainside Hospital after my follow up visit with Dr. Staten. She encourages me again to attend the next couple of group sessions she's holding this month. On my way home I figured I'd hit the Target SuperCenter in Clark to pick up some basic toiletries or a few knick-knacks, like tuna, Soy Milk and Honey Nut Cheerios. Since the incident two weeks ago my cupboards are bare which doesn't necessarily bother me. Eating is the last thing on my mind. All I do is think about Brian, every minute.

There is back to back traffic, all of us squashed together like the stick of gum in the side pocket of my Guess denim skinny jeans. I keep a stick of gum, and some tic-tac's to freshen my breath in case Brian pops over to check in on me. Which he doesn't. Who would blame him after the stunt I pulled kicking him out and cursing his mother for no good reason? Hanging out with Dr. Staten I'm learning what's really going on. It's me. I'm at fault. Or as Dr. Staten puts it, "Its fear Arianna. Plain old fear of loss or rejection. You are stronger than you think." Easier said than done, doctor.

I turn the radio on and switch it to K-LOVE 106.9 FM; then, 107.9 WPPZ-FM flip flopping back and forth between two contemporary gospel channels. I'm not sure if Brandon Heath's "I'm Not Who I Was" or Erika Campbell's "A Little More Jesus" most accurately convey what I'm feeling at this moment; I settle on Brandon. Cause I'm not sure who I am or ever knew who I was. I really hope the lyricist can help me figure it out.

I'm sitting in traffic- total gridlock. The woman in the funky red Prism directly in front of me spends more time using her rearview

26

mirror to apply mascara and clownish red lipstick than driving her car through the open pockets in the lane to her left. If she moves up, I can squeeze into a space behind her. "Come on lady, move it or lose it!" I tap the button to roll down my window to scream out. "I have to be somewhere!" Not true. Anything is better than being stuck in the same place. Waiting has never been my strong suit.

The sudden buzzing sound interrupts my ranting. I notice my iPhone, housed in my cup holder, vibrates. I quickly glance down to read it; then, back up at the traffic filled highway, "Don't you dare cry!" I bang my hands on the steering wheel. "C'mon, pull it together. Don't you dare cry Arianna, not one tear girl!"

I repeat after reading Brian's text:
Hey. It's been a minute. Just checkin' in. Still, not sure abt being in luv, but I do a luv u. Hope ur doing ok. BM <3

"I hate that I need you so much Bri!" I wail. "And no matter what you text. You don't love me. There's nothing worth loving. It's probably indigestion you're feeling and you just think it's love. Indigestion isn't love!" I wipe the fog off my glasses and huff out a whimper. "Stop it Arianna!" I tell myself. "Stop it. Why can't you trust him? Why can't you be happy?"

I push the phone away as hard as I can; instead of responding and wipe the tears from my cheeks.

It vibrates again, and I unconsciously read it:
Have u decided not to talk to me? BM <3

I toss the phone into the empty passenger seat, and stare at it for a few seconds. The tears run down the side of my face and chin which I brush off with the collar of my shirt. The stream slips faster and faster down my cheeks covering my nose and mouth as if something's suffocating me. I can barely see. I roll down the window, poke my face out and pray for a small gust of air. My head throbs as the thoughts of me and Brian occupy my mind.

I withdraw back in my seat when I notice a passenger in the car next to me staring in my direction. She looks at me and mouths, "Are you ok?" I nod and give her half a smile.

"Just stop talking to me," I say out loud grabbing my forehead and shaking it to try to calm the inchoate diatribe of momentary tête-à-têtes of Brian Maxwell. Then, I decided to take the exit for Cranford in the opposite direction of the Superstore. I need to be somewhere pleasant. I pulled up into the driveway of the two story beige Colonial with red trim. The tall lush emerald arborvitae trees line the front of the house as a privacy screen.

I proceed up the driveway, slowly, stopping midway to send a text: **Hey Auntie M- You home? I'm outside. A-**

A few seconds later my cell vibrates: **No sweetie. We're shopping. R U ok? Be home in 30. Wait for us? Garage door is unlocked.**

I back out of the driveway and hop back on the parkway. I skip the superstore and spend the rest of my long drive home, glum. Then I started thinking, attending a few group sessions was probably not a bad idea.

3

TIMOTHY

∞**"YOU DON'T LISTEN."**

"What do you mean, Tim?"

"If you'd be quiet, let me speak. I'll tell you," he snaps.

"I'm listening. I want to understand. I want to make you happy."

"Happy? I'd be happy if I could find an equal. A strong woman who knows her place? Who understands her role?"

"I can be that for you. I can play any role you like."

"Yet you don't. You don't play well in my world which makes you less than me. Just get out of my face."

"I'm sorry, Tim," she says. By this time, she is crying which makes him even angrier than before. It shows her frailty.

"I'm just tired of you, Melissa and having to fix the things you mess up. Are you trying to purposely agitate me?" She stood in front of him in a fitted red dress, showing all her curves, a pair of golden lace-up open-toe shoes, and the heels were too high to be worn alone. Even her curly hair hanging over her shoulders and kissing her neck is tempting.

"I'm sorry. Very sorry. What can I do to fix this?"

"Don't you understand I'm trying to love you and I expect more from you? We are supposed to be a team, right? And you know, I can't stand to have anyone else look at you that way. Why can't you show some discretion? But you just have to keep on disrespecting me by flaunting yourself around my friends like a whore!"

"I didn't mean to flaunt myself," she sobs. "I wore this dress for you. I'm sorry!"

"You are always sorry, Melissa. You always want to fix things after the fact and then never mean to do anything. Yet you keep on flirting with stupid. When are you going to act like a lady with some common sense?"

Timothy doesn't understand why Melissa brings out this side of him. Why so much rage? He tries to be a better person, but his anger rules; similar to how his father's anger ruled every time he beat his mother- which Timothy hates. When it came to his mother, his father didn't only beat her physically, but his words were her crushing and to her detriment. Now, Timothy is behaving just like him. His father would come home and slap his mother around for no good reason.

"My mom was just weak!" He says it aloud without realizing it. He squirms in his seat 'till he finds a position that doesn't cause his lower back to ache or legs to tingle.

"Why do you think your mother was the weak one?" She asks.

"What do you mean?" He returns his focus to Dr. Staten; for a moment he has forgotten that he is in her office still lying on the cushy burgundy lounge chaise.

"Well, some people would say that a man slapping a woman is an act of cowardice. Do you agree with that?" She sits upright and leans toward him.

"I think it depends on what you are calling weak. I mean she was too weak to leave him and too frail to fight back. Some days I would jump in- you know- right in the middle of them. Standing toe to toe with him. I thought I was strong." Timothy shifts in the chair. "I would get right up in his face and try to fight him." He pops upright, leans in toward Dr. Staten glaring into her dark brown eyes with daubs of light brown flecks. "When I was younger, he would just toss me aside then beat me down—stomp me like I was a man. I wasn't though I was just a kid!"

"Exactly, you were just a kid. Did it take real strength for him to toss you around or slap your mother?" She refuses to retreat from her position.

"No." Timothy leans back on the lounge to escape the now uncomfortable closeness. His eyes wander the huge office in search of a new focus; something other than Dr. Staten's scrutinizing gaze. They pass over the oak shelf full of medical books, a half-open cherry wood armoire with stacks of paper seeping through the door, and the glass fish tank with coral stones, mismatched sea shells, and multi-colored pebbles lining the bottom. There is one fattened marbled fish soaring back and forth from one end of the tank to the other. They come to rest at a picture sitting on her desk of a smiling Dr. Staten nestled between the arms of an older man and woman who seem equally happy. "So as soon as I got big enough, strong enough- I got him."

"How did that play out? Tell me what happened?"

"How does dredging up the past help me stop from slapping the stupidity out of my lady?"

"Why don't we talk it through and see?"

"Talking has never been a strength of mine. I come from a family that strikes first, yells second but lacks the ability to converse. That's why, I don't understand how replaying my childhood is helpful." Timothy grimaces. He knows where the conversation is leading. And he is not excited about going through the archives of his mind.

"You have to get to the root of the problem in order to fix it, Timothy," Dr. Staten says while clasping his hand with her long skinny fingers. "And that can be an unsettling process."

"Well I don't remember everything."

"Just after you told me what happened between you and your girlfriend, Melissa, you brought up your mother and started talking about a time when you 'got back' at your father. Why don't we start there?"

"It was long ago."

"Try to think back." He doesn't look at her; instead, he concentrates on the framed picture and wonders how beautiful it would be to paint. He takes a deep breath, closing his eyes a minute. "He came home from work. She had cleaned the kitchen, you know."

"Your mother right?"

"Yes." He says sharply.

"Ok I'm just trying to make sure I keep up with you." Timothy appreciates her trying to understand. He eases back into the chair and calms his tone. "Anyway she'd cleaned the living room, made dinner for him and had a beer in the fridge nicely chilled. Everything she thought he wanted. Everything he said he needed. He came in the door and it was like he was going through a checklist of reasons not to beat her: house clean- check, floors swept- check, kids sitting around doing their homework- check and kids being quiet- double check. All good she thought. She made sure to clean everything up to the standard that he liked and he didn't complain. Next he went to the kitchen and looked around. Kitchen clean- check, the aroma of dinner in the air- check, nothing burnt- double check. Then he pulled the chair up to the table and sat down. Whew the coast is clear—." He wipes his brow, as he relives the day.

"She put the plate in front of him, napkin in his lap- fork to the left and knife and spoon to the right. He picked up the fork and bit a piece of the fried chicken- we both inhaled. He didn't yell so he must've liked it- we both exhaled. But then it happened, he scooped up some peas.... they were too cold! They had been sitting out on the table too long I guess. Who beats a woman for an hour over cold peas?" Dr. Staten motions for him to continue. He is glad she understands it's rhetorical. She sits in silence listening non-judgmentally, which makes him feel better.

"My dad, that's who!" He slams his hand on the arm of the seat and the thump of the wood echoes through the cushions. "I was only 18 and I didn't understand. You don't beat a person over peas," his voice raises with each word, "She could have quickly put them in the microwave or even cooked a whole new bag of frozen peas with smoked turkey for flavor like he liked. Or, she could have driven down the block to the *Ole Southern Spot* restaurant and bought a large side of peas in the time it took him to drag her around the once clean living room smudging my Mother's bloody face across the oak floor and cutting her legs- stripping them to the bone on the glass from the smashed plate of good smelling, but apparently too cold peas!"

"What did you do?" Dr. Staten asks with her hands clasped tightly.

"I hit him! While he was dragging her- I jumped on him and grabbed his face and hit him, repeatedly. I picked up a handful of peas off the floor and shoved them in his mouth. Then while he was down I stomped him- like he'd stomped her. And I went to the kitchen table to use the knife that had been on the right side of the now missing and shattered plate. I was going to stab him till he bled out." He takes a deep breath. His heart pounding as he blows out one thunderous breath, "Then I heard it. She says: *NO... don't kill him Tim! Put it down or I'm going to have you locked up!* Bloody and bruised, she musters the strength to pick up the telephone to call the police on me!"

I say to her, *"Wow, you're going to call the police on me?"*

"He's my husband."

"Yes, I can see how he's a great catch."

"Tim, I love him!"

"Love. And, I suppose he loves you too?"

"He does. He just needs help. What kind of wife would I be, if I left him at his worst?"

"Got it. But you'd be more convincing if your face wasn't jacked or you weren't bleeding to death in need of stitches because the love of your life was served lukewarm peas! Man, I'm out."

"Wait Tim ...just help me get him to the couch."

∞∞∞∞

"I couldn't believe her words. Beyond stupid is all I could think. Then I tell her, she doesn't need me, "let love carry him to the couch." He hunches his shoulder, "I end it by saying, I just hope love doesn't kill you when he comes too."

"Timothy, what did you want her to say?"

"Something that makes sense. Show an inkling of strength"

"What did you need her to do?"

"Anything. Anything- but that. How about take us and leave!" He tries to suck the taste of disgust out of his mouth.

"What happened after that?" She asks.

"I stepped over that woman and her husband and walked out the door. After that day, I only came home to sleep and eat till I saved up enough money to pay the college fees my scholarship didn't cover so I could get out of that house."

"Is that when you started looking at women differently?"

35

"Not necessarily but that's when I realized two things; one, you don't get in the business between a man and his woman- cause she'll always pick him and two, women are weak."

"All women? Is that your opinion, Timothy?" Dr. Staten grabs a pen and scribbles some notes in her blue notepad.

"You know what's wrong with treating women, good?" He smirks.

"What Timothy?"

"It's unfamiliar to them. So, I give them what they know."

"And your Dad, what did you realize about him?" Dr. Staten stops writing and looks up at him.

"What do you mean?" He turns from her and pans the room again.

"Well it seems you've put a lot of thought into what women are and how women respond. You've based this decision on how your mother responds or reacts to your father. I'm assuming you put the same level of forethought into men. What about your, Father? What revelation did you come to about men?"

Timothy sits there. He has no response. He's spent his life's energy on his mother. It never occurred to him to put any effort thinking about his father. He has made it a point to never think about him.

"Is it time to go? Are we done?" He asks.

"Are you ready to go?"

He looks at Dr. Staten; then, over to her desk again, at a framed picture he assumes is of Dr. Staten with her parents.

"Are those your parents?" He points at the picture.

"Yes. You didn't answer my question."

"That's a really nice picture."

"Thank you."

"You should have a family portrait done instead of a photograph, though."

"Perhaps in the future. Back to my question. What did you realize about your father?" She still waits though no response. Timothy sits silently, staring back at her.

"Well then I'll take your silence to mean you want this session to be over." Dr. Staten taps her pen on the desk. "We can pick up the conversation from here next time. Before you head out I wanted to let you know that I'm starting group sessions."

Timothy rolls his eyes, rubs his sweaty hands onto his pant legs, grabs his coat and magazine as he stands.

"Wait a minute Timothy. I know that look. Give it a chance. I think you'll like the other person. She's nice."

"She?" He asks. "I should have known."

"Just promise you'll come to at least one group session? It will be a good opportunity for you to meet with other people who face similar struggles."

"I'll think about it. When is it anyway?"

"On Friday the 19th."

"You know I have a ton of work. I'm going to be tied up for months working on my exhibit at Princeton."

"Oh yes." Dr. Staten taps her pen against the arm of her chestnut chair. "I remember it's going to be at your alma mater Princeton University. Are you working on a lot of new pieces?"

"Yeah." He looks down at her seated in the chair. "I mean yes. I've been working on some real strong pieces but I kind of hit a lull."

"Don't worry about it. Maybe group meetings will help motivate you. Thinking about something other than your craft may prove to be a good distraction" Dr. Staten smirks. "The sessions are going to be Friday evenings. You can make it one Friday right?"

"I'll see. This exhibit is taking up a lot of my time. I've been working on this one piece for months now. Ever since I started meeting with you."

"Nice. Then the more sessions you come to the more inspiration." She looks at him with kind eyes. "I can't wait to see it."

Timothy thinks her kind eyes liven up the room. They also have a weird calming affect on him.

"Ok. I guess if you can come to my show. I can spare a Friday or two."

"Great I will have my secretary call you to confirm as we get closer to the date okay?"

"Okay Doc." Timothy turns to walk out of her office.

"Timothy," she says.

He stops.

"Don't think I'll forget about the question I asked you earlier that you never answered."

"I know. Later Doc. I have to sleep on that one—too much too soon. Hell, you should be glad you got the 'peas' story outta me. I haven't shared that in," Timothy pauses, leans his head to the side and looks up, squinting his eyes and pursing his lips. "Man, never. I usually leave it all on the canvas."

"Ah your paintings- That's where your muse hides."

"Later Doc," he says with a smirk and walks out.

4

WON'T LET GO

∞**TIMOTHY PACED, BACK** and forth in his living room for about five minutes, smashing the plush gray carpet underfoot with every footprint before he walked toward the front door. *Stuffy in here.* Outside there's a distinct smell of pesticide sprays, fertilizer, and mulch coming from his neighbor's crisply sculptured lawn. He covers his nose to mask the smell. It's a dry quiet day. The golden sun tries to push its way past a greyish blue cloud. "Ugh looks like rain, it's going to be a gloomy day," he mumbles. To the right of him is two gleaming, jet-black Mercedes cluttering his neighbors' driveway. To the left there's a Bumble-Bee colored Hummer, and a silver Porsche. He glances at his Polaris white Jaguar and smiles. Looking down his pristine tree-lined street full of lavish homes, fancy cars, and manicured lawns, he whispers, "Success. I have finally arrived!" He inhales again, exhales, then closes the door.

He trails across the white porcelain foyer to a grand, dark cherry wood spiral staircase. The white wood railing spans the front of the entryway. He looks up at the grand staircase winding its way toward the back bedrooms stretching his neck to see if Melissa left the back bedroom light on. *Nope, good- she remembered.*

Walking through the house brings back memories of the early days. The large house was drab and cold when he first purchased it. Room after room had morgue like features, with white walls everywhere as if previously inhabited by zombies. Six months, he spent working on it adding a splash of color here and there- until it became home. Timothy ends up in the immaculately clean living room with the plush buff carpet from end to end, stopping to stare at his portraiture. In it, a man grabs hold of a boy who's slipping off the edge of a huge mountain dotted with patches of green shrubs.

The boy's honey brown hands clasp the man's dark mahogany arm with the man's other hand he stretches to secure a hold to the boy's chest. Sweat dripping off his face, he grits his teeth and with a look of yearning mixed with utter determination, he holds on. The intensity of the visual draws Timothy into the painting, every time. The artwork titled, *WON'T LET GO*, is one of his first pieces. He ends up in front of the painting in ritualistic meditations. It's a personification of a Father's love. Since it is the one thing he wishes exists for him, Timothy creates a world where it does.

His stroll turns into a heavy pace, back and forth, then, again back and forth. Every few steps he pauses and huffs. Pacing with iPhone in hand, he dials the same seven digits three times; then hangs up.

"Fourth time's a charm." He encourages himself to let the call go through. "You didn't tell me we were meeting in a church, Doc." He squeezes his iPhone tight, rubs the sweat off the phone onto his Valentino distressed straight fit jeans.

"Timothy is that you?" Dr. Staten asks.

"Yes."

"Why is meeting in a church a problem?"

"I didn't say that." He quickly moves the phone from his ear and frowns at it. In that moment he contemplates hanging up. "I mean, not really it's just....telling all my personal business about me, my lady, my moms and pops, in the church house- seems crazy-."

"Why does it seem crazy to you?" The tone in her voice rises and falls when she speaks.

He thinks Dr. Staten's on the other end of the line laughing at him. "I don't seem anything, especially crazy. I'm not crazy Doc," he says sharply.

"I know that."

"Then why did you call me crazy?"

"You realize I did not say you were crazy. I repeated your comment about meeting in a church house- *seeming crazy*. So I'm asking. Why do you feel the idea of holding our session at a church seems crazy?"

He is quiet. He wishes he hadn't let the call go through or better still that he never dialed her number the fourth time.

"Okay Timothy- why don't we back up a little bit and start the conversation from another point?"

Timothy stops pacing and plops down on his soft green Italian Leather couch draped with a colorful Ghanaian Kente cloth throw and huffs. When he lands, the cold leather crunches.

"Who told you we are holding the session in a church?" She asks.

"Your secretary!"

"Oh so you spoke with Diane and she told you that the location of our next session is going to be at the church?"

"No!" He grunts.

"Oh then please explain."

"She left me a message with the address of our meeting location and I recognized it." He leans back against the green sofa.

"How did you recognize it?"

"I recognized it because-"

"You don't live anywhere near there." She interrupts him.

He says curtly. "I go to that church"

He looks at the phone and cringes even though he knows she cannot see him. There is a long pause, and the deafening silence makes him nervous. He wonders if now Dr. Staten is annoyed.

"Mr. Timothy Fox," she begins, "do you mean to tell me that you are calling me to complain about having a session at a church you already attend?"

When he hears the puzzlement in her voice, he thinks deciding to call her was a mistake.

He props himself up on the sofa, "I'm saying-- that's weird." He pauses. "I just hope the Pastor's wife isn't the person you said is joining me for a group session," then continues playfully. "You know Doc, God don't like ugly." He laughs.

"Well Timothy if that's your only concern then you have nothing to worry about. Mrs. Jacobs will not be joining our sessions. And the session after that will be at my office. We'll probably meet in my office more than at the church. It just depends on my hospital rounds. I think you and God will be fine. How does that sound?" She says.

He loosens his grip on the phone when he hears her smile coming through her playful words.

43

"Whew, perfect. Cause I have enough to deal with as it is."

"I will see you on Friday, Timothy."

"Keep smiling Doc. See you Friday." When he tries to hang up, the iPhone clings to his sweaty ear. He wipes the sweat off his ear with his shoulder, swipes the sleek black iPhone on his pant leg then drops it on the long glass coffee table in front of him.

As he replays the conversation with Dr. Staten, he laughs at the thought of it and marvels at her inner strength. She's so cool helping him become a cool man too instead of the emotionally stunted, angry man he is now. He's desperately trying not to repeat the sins of his father. Every so often after talking with her, he sees a glimmer of hope.

Before he can clear the couch his phone rings, "Hey doc," he quickly taps the speakerphone to answer, "You forgot something?"

"Doc? This is not the doctor, Timothy. It's your mother." Timothy drops the phone and immediately wishes he had sent the call to his voicemail. When it falls, it makes a large *CLANG* as it hits the end of the glass table.

"Timothy!" His mother, calls. "Are you still there? Why are you seeing a doctor son? Are you okay?"

He hears his mother's voice crisply through his phone's speaker. It makes his heart race and body stiffen, as if to brace for an impending crash. She has a peculiar way of making a campground in his mind and lingers there. He knows the conversation is going to get far worse before it gets better.

"Timothy! Timothy, are you going to answer me?" She keeps repeating it.

He taps the speakerphone off and puts the phone to his ear. "Yes I'm here. You don't have to keep calling me, I can hear you perfectly." It amazes him how he goes from speaking comfortable slang to more proper lending great concern to word choice, pronunciation, and grammar while speaking with her.

"Mother, what do you want?" he says coldly.

"You're my only son dear. I just called to check in. Unfortunately this is the only way we speak to one another- since you never call or come home anymore."

"You have two other children, Mother." He takes a deep breath. "I am fine. I do not call because I have nothing new to convey."

"Yes but you are my only son, Timothy," she replies. "Anyway your father and I miss you tremendously."

He scoffs under his breath at the mention of his father, sucking his teeth and shaking his head at the phone.

"Timothy, did you hear me? Oh wait a minute." There's a pause. "Your father wants to speak with you."

"What?" He can feel the knots swelling up in his belly which is obviously an indication, he is not ready for this conversation.

"Hey son," his father calls. Timothy doesn't answer right away. It seems to him, the room is hotter and more constrictive than before the call. He checks his pulse and rubs his forehead.

"Hey boy, did ya hear me speaking to you?" his father calls again.

"Yes I can hear you," Timothy says short and quick. He keeps the phone pressed securely against his ear, remaining still and barely breathing. He sits on the couch, holding his breath for a moment while inwardly praying this conversation will end.

"Well me and your Ma want to see you more often. You know you shouldn't forget your family and where you come from, boy"

"Well I could never forget *you* or my mother." Timothy smirks. "You know especially with all the wonderful childhood memories you created. You know what I mean?" He wishes there was a way his words could come across colder.

"You startin' on me boy? I'm just trying to have a civil conversation with you. Before I can get a decent word out edgewise here you go fightin' me!" His father snaps.

"Ah there he is."

"Who? Whatchu mean?"

"I knew the real you would show up any minute now. You know a father shouldn't have to try to act civil with his child. He should already *be* civilized. If she wants to play pretend house with you that is none of my affair. I'm not going to sit here and act like you are the Father of the Year. You're not!"

"Well you comin' over or not? Your Moms would really like to see you. I don't have time to argue with my own blood. Here, speak to her about the particulars."

"Oh particulars, huh?"

"Yeah that's what I said!"

"I guess my mother has been working with you like one of the students from her little English class. Particular is that the vocabulary word of the week. Very good sir. Can you spell it?" He snickers. Timothy's sharp tongue is purposeful.

"You laughin' at me? You laughin' at me boy? My own blood." His father squawks. "Here Prissy take this phone I'm trying. He ain't!"

"Good bye, it's been *particularly* uneventful speaking with you," Timothy's voice is calm and steady. This time, he smiles gleefully. He is mostly pleased with himself, aside from the one time he raised his voice, he was cool and collected. "Checkmate," he whispers.

"Timothy," an irritatingly soft voice calls to him.

He eases his grip on the phone, sitting back against the sofa, fuming.

"You know you don't have to be combative with your father. He is trying. It took a lot for him to come to the phone and express his feelings. It took a lot for him to ask you to come home for a visit." His mother says.

He takes the phone from his ear. He closes his eyes softly counting *one, two, three* and exhales.

"We both really miss you and we want you to come over for dinner one night soon. That is all we are asking. I do not believe that is too much to ask of you. Promise me son."

He can hear the hint of desperation in her voice which makes him angry. She has none of Dr. Staten's inner strength. At this point, he knows, if he doesn't get off the phone with her soon, he'll implode.

"Okay. Yes. Sure. Anything. Fine." He blurts out. "I will come over for dinner one weekend soon. Now may I go? I have a ton of things to do. And before you ask, yes it is work related. Yes, I'm still painting every day. And yes, I will try to call more often," he answers before she can ask. "Okay. I have to go!"

"Timothy I lov-"

He quickly presses the red symbol to hang up before she has a chance to utter the four letter word 'L O V E' he feels has landed him on Dr. Staten's burgundy lounger. The weekly sessions as confirmation that he'll continue. He rushes to the other side of his living room. Heart throbbing and panting he stares at his meditative painting of the father and son. One, two, three, he pounds his fist into his palm. One, two, three, he shakes his hands to relieve the stinging pulse from his earlier blows. One, two, three, he repeats it until his pulse steadies. One, two, three, he says one last time until he is completely calm. Standing there staring at the father and son portrait, Timothy hopes to get to the point where he doesn't detest the sound of his mother's voice, taunts his father or boils over in uncontrollable rage whenever he speaks with them. He holds fast to the notion that maybe one day he'll see the determination, commitment, and love portrayed in this living room canvas in his father's eyes. "This is a self-portrait, this is a self-portrait," he mumbles twice.

5

GROUP SESSION

∞ **"THERE'S THIS POEM** I came across while rummaging through some old books in this vintage corner bookstore called *Angles of Perception*. Somedays I recite it. Do you want to hear it?" I ask.

When Dr. Staten remains quiet, I go for it.
One family
Two Children.
A father. A mother.
The broom is cracked
The basin is broken
The World has a lightning storm
Walking the corner
At the market down the block,
In the school yard
A lightning storm,
Until sleet, snow
Wind, rain
Hail, black ice
Take me home
From the portal
From which they came,
This is the model family

"What do you like about that poem? It seems rather bleak." Dr. Staten asks.
"Bleak?"
"Yes."

"No, not bleak- truthful."

"How so?"

I pause for a few minutes. "Do you think a person can ever really be whole?"

"Are you changing the subject, Arianna?"

"If someone has been broken into a thousand pieces, can they ever piecemeal their life back together?" I continued. Dr. Staten is always asking me to share and now when I want to share something, she interrupts me.

"Well what do you think?" She turns toward me unnervingly close. A bad habit of hers. I guess she decided to let me win this one. She has a bad habit of sitting unnervingly close though, invading my space.

"I'm not sure how it can ever really be possible." I squirm in my seat to lessen the grip of her cold stare. "But at least I am hopeful, which is one place I have never been before," I give her what I feel is a weird smile. The left side of my mouth sort of curves up.

"That's good Arianna. What about being whole gives you pause?"

"Can you back up a little?" I ask. Which she does, giving me a chance to escape her gaze. "So many things give me pause."

"Like what?" Dr. Staten asks.

"Some days I sit in the dark remembering the pain. It plagues me; then, I think what can I do to stop remembering? Or at least trade it in for something new." I lean back in the constricting rickety old wooden chair. I slide my hand up the side of the chair leg, stopping to caress each groove that makes up this masterfully created antique.

"What kind of pain is plaguing you?"

"All kinds."

"Will you elaborate a little more?"

Her persistence is notable. Although, I have already proven, I can be more evasive than she can persist. "Nope," I say.

"Ok how about we come back to that question? Can you tell me this, what do you do when the pain gets unbearable?"

"How long have you had this chair?" I look down at the chair. I slide my hand up and down the right side of it too its leg. "It must be an antique because no one puts the time in to make furniture like this anymore. Everything is factory-made. The architect of this chair cared... no loved this chair."

"Arianna, will you answer my question?"

"I mean this is handmade. No way, it's manufactured. Feel the grooves on the side," I reach for Dr. Staten's hand. She rejects me. Which doesn't bother me, surprisingly. "They remind me of cuts. Not the ones I'm used to. Every one of these incises are necessary. Look at the distressed color of the wood. Someone labored to strip, scrape, tarnish and rub to make it perfect."

"Arianna, why is the chair so important to you?"

I am silent.

"Do you see yourself?"

"Sort of," I whisper "I remember a time."

"What time? What do you remember? Would you like to tell me about it?"

"It was long ago. I had a moment of happiness with my Mom before she left me." I mutter.

"Ah your mother." Dr. Staten pulls out a little blue note pad and scribbles something on the pages.

"What are you writing in that book?" I say sharply.

"They are my notes. I write things down I don't want to forget. Really so I don't miss anything you share with me."

"Do you always take notes on me?"

"No, not always. Does my writing bother you? I can show you if you'd like?"

"No!" I blurt out. "I mean no- just wanted to know it all," I feel uneasy considering I brought up the subject in the first place. I have to learn how to watch my reactions. I turn away from her and stare out the window.

"Arianna," she calls me, "do you want to tell me about the *happy moment* with your Mother?"

Her big bright eyes intently looking at me seem genuine and strong. Two things I am not. I definitely hadn't planned to tell her anything substantive about my parents. Not today. But from the moment I sit in the rickety old chair, the flashbacks begin. I realize this is the first time my mind has been free of thoughts of Brian. *That's unbelievable.*

"I was sitting at the kitchen table in a light brown oak chair between my cousins, Alex and Alexis getting ready to eat dinner. Our golden retriever is lying next to us. The shiny yellow walls were too bright to look at long without its brightness hurting your eyes. It made the kitchen seem like the largest room in the house. In the middle of the kitchen sat a large brown hickory table with chairs like these." I point at the wooden chair. "I would jab designs into the wood with my knife and fork to keep busy."

Dr. Staten looks at me with her inquisitive eyes, so I continue.

"I can hear the crackling of chicken sizzling in the black cast iron frying pan. My belly gurgles when the smells of macaroni and cheese, cornbread and candied yams seep through the oven door. My mother places three steaming plates and a glass of milk in front of us. The macaroni oozing with cheese, the yams stuck together by chunks of cinnamon and sugar, collard greens with smoked turkey bones sticking up out of them and the cornbread sweet and corny with extra butter. Every smell is dancing in front of my nose."

"Okay that sounds scrumptious! Children notice everything, don't you think?" She asks me.

A question I ignore.

"My Mother plops down at the end of the table wiping the sweat from her brow. Her other hand tracing her leg down the side of her thigh, stopping to caress her ankle, and then to massage her foot. She has no idea of the amount of chaos we were about to get into." I chuckle. "My cousin Alex was sneaking a chicken bone under the table to my golden retriever, when Alexis reached over me to grab a chicken wing off his plate. Her scrawny elbow knocked over my milk glass. It pools on the table, branching into two trails, one heading for the plate of cornbread and the other my lap. I quickly push my chair from the table, which shrieks as it slides against the cherry wood floor. A loud thump echoes from it when Alex hits it. My mother raced to chase the trail with two pale green dish rags. Her hands are straddling the table."

"It's amazing how fast everyone can move!" She says.

I nod, so she doesn't derail my story. "Alex's deep brown-eyed stare was constant. He places his hand on the rim of his glass rocking it, taunting her, then toppling it over. The milk splashes onto the cornbread and his half eaten macaroni and cheese. I looked at Alexis nodded; her beckoning eyes told me to finish the milk bath. Alex smirks. So, I look up at my mother, her red eyes, disheveled hair, preoccupied wet hands, and heavy breathing aids in my decision. I shrug my shoulders and push the last milk glass over."

"Wow Arianna! What a mess." Dr. Staten gasps. "Did this really happen?"

"Yes!" I start laughing. "The kitchen was a shambles. It reeked! I cover my mouth to make sure no laughter escapes as a puddle of milk grows in my lap. Alex hid under the table next to our retriever. Alexis put the chicken wing back onto his plate. Then, my mother-" I pause.

"Yes, what happened next?" Dr. Staten asked, her mouth half open.

I engage her enthusiasm by making my voice crescendo from a whisper to a boisterous voice back to a whisper. "She lifts the soaking dishcloths dripping like little white raindrops onto the table and tosses it behind her into the white porcelain sink. She plops back down onto her chair, covers her face with her wet hands and laughs. In a laugh that commands all the space. Her face was as red as a beet. Then she opens her arms, disregarding the chaos of the dinner table and beckons us to come. We all found refuge nestled in the crevice of her arms and inhaling the aroma of her essence." I look down at the ground and inhale. "She smelled of lilies, flour, oil, cheese, chicken, yams, sweat and milk."

"That was probably the most special smell around." Dr. Staten says.

"Yes it was." I sink back into my chair, "Wow, I can't believe I remember it, like it was yesterday." I work my fingers through the grooves of the chair leg again. "I haven't thought about that house in years."

"Well, that's one amazing story, Arianna. You and your cousins, Alex and Alexis must be close?"

"Yes. Yes we were. For a little while, that is."

"Where are they now? And your dog?"

"Sam." I smile. "That's my dog's name—well...was his name. I forgot to tell you. He's gone. My cousins moved down south, I think. To be honest I'm not sure. I haven't spoken to them since I moved out years ago."

"Oh your aunt and uncle raised you, after your parents passed?"

Immediately, I look down at the floor because I can feel a cry coming. Why am I such a cry baby? I refuse to let a tear slip down the side of my cheek. I try to think happy thoughts. But, I know, if I say this next sentence, that's it, they'll be no holding back; I'm going to wail. *Don't say it aloud, Arianna.*

"Yeah, everyone I love leaves." I say and immediately start crying. Dr. Staten has taken a lot from me today. I can't give her any more truth. I can't pour out another part of me. *How can talking about a bit of happiness make me cry?*

"It's okay. Let it out, Arianna?" Dr. Staten scoots next to me. "You've been holding on to so much for so long."

I don't understand it. All this drivel is making me cross. No matter how hard I try, the tears keep coming. They drip off my face and onto the floor faster than I can wipe them away. I keep my head down though deep inside, I know there's no avoiding Dr. Staten. She is not going to let up. She's going to ride this moment as if a jockey rides a thoroughbred in the Kentucky Derby.

"Does this chair remind you of the chair in your old house?"

Here she goes again. The great doctor coaxed me into a deeper revelation. "Yes. No one has loved me that much in a long time." Why do you keep answering her? Just shut up. I think to myself.

"What about your Aunt and Uncle? Or Brian even? It seems they love you. Why won't you let Brian see you distressed, full of jabs- like the chair you covet? Or tired and disheveled like your mother." Once again, she's sitting uncomfortably close. She's on the edge of her seat. One good breeze will blow her right onto the floor. Which selfishly, at this particular moment, would be helpful. Laughing at her is better than being her thoroughbred.

"What do you know about him?" I bark at her. If I can't laugh, I'll have to rely on my anger. "What do you know about anything except what I choose to tell you from time to time?"

"I see you, Arianna." She must have some weird ogling fetish that makes her gawking acceptable. "You're not alone. I'm here to help you understand something very important."

"What?" I wipe away the lingering tears on my cheeks.

"You are loved." She hugs me this time. Squeezing too tight. I can only inhale. There's not enough space between us for the air to let out a real exhale. I wish she'd let go.

"And broken into a thousand pieces," I wiggle free of her grip.

"Maybe so but don't forget, hopeful. Which is powerful. One day all of a sudden, you'll find each broken piece fits like a puzzle into a marvelous recreation."

I get up from the rickety old chair and make a dash for the long burgundy lounger across the room. She doesn't follow me. I like that. Most people would immediately ask questions like, why did you move? Where are you going? Or try another hug. Not her. She knows her limitations. How to let a person be whatever they choose. I sit in my chair. She sits in hers, and we wait. For a moment, silence is our friend.

"Arianna, I'd like to invite you to attend group sessions." Dr. Staten says. "There is another individual, a young man who I've been meeting with as well. I think you two would fare well meeting together."

I am quiet.

"Are you up to it?"

"No, but I guess there's no turning back now." I say sinking deeper into the lounge chaise.

6

GROUP SESSION

∞**"FIRST OF ALL,** it's great that you both have been attending our group sessions. There are two or three others who keep meaning to join us but they have yet to make it here. I'm sure when they're ready, they'll be here. Hats off to the two of you for being so courageous. It takes courage to share in a group and go through the healing journey together." Dr. Staten says to me and Timothy, the young man sitting next to me. "That being said, Arianna," she glances at me, "after weeks of meeting, is there something you'd like to share about the marks on your arms and wrist?"

I look at Dr. Staten and Timothy. When it comes to sharing, I am conflicted. Part of me wants to talk about the cuts. A larger part, deep down in the war zone called my mind, is terrified of the idea of letting anyone that close to me. I don't understand how opening this door is a good thing. How will it help? How can anything I say in this room help me get back to Brian? So, I just sit in my 'happy mommy moment'- staring toward an empty spot in the corner of the room, defenseless. Hoping the pitifulness of my expression is enough for Dr. Staten to give me a pass and leave me alone.

"Well Arianna," Dr. Staten probes.

"Well what?"

"What do you think?"

"About what?"

"Anything? Anything, you want to share about the marks?"

"You mean share with y'all?" I nod toward Timothy. "How long have we been doing this?"

"Doing what, Arianna?"

"You know...*this*," I pointed around the room. "Coming here. Talking to you. *Sharing*?"

"Why do you ask?"

"Why don't you answer?" Dr. Staten stares at me with her lips pursed and squinted eyes. "I'm trying to measure- if enough time has passed for me to be this open."

"How do you possibly measure something like that?"

"It's like a comfort meter."

"What are the parameters of this meter? Does it depend on the number of visits to trigger it?"

"Something like that."

"Something like that- can you elaborate?"

"I don't know how to explain it. But It's how I am. It's my process."

"We all have a process. I can't fault you for that." Dr. Staten pauses. "Um. Alright, we have been meeting for over a month. Where does that fit into your comfort meter?"

"I'm still processing. Why can't we let Timothy talk?" I say awkwardly.

"Uh-uh. I shared already, Arianna, remember? It's your turn, lady." Timothy replies quickly.

I look at Timothy sitting on the wooden stool, swiveling back and forth, smirking mischievously. His dark smooth skin and muscular frame make him more appealing than I care to admit. He's cultured, intelligent and artistic. If he weren't as screwed up as me, meeting weekly in this cave with a head doctor, who makes us relive our past struggles- while exploiting our inability to act normally; I would definitely be attracted to him. Then, there's my never ending love-lust novella for Brian. Moreover, on second thought, I realize this guy wouldn't stand a chance with me, not when Brian Maxwell is out there.

"You mean the cuts?" I blurt it out, quickly. "No need to act like the elephant is not in the room." Timothy and I do somewhat of a chuckle that lessens the tension that grows more and more obvious in our inner circle.

"Well alright then. Yes the cuts Arianna," Dr. Staten asks.

"What about them?"

"Tell me how you came about cutting yourself? When did it start?"

"You know I have parents, right?"

"Arianna you're evading." Dr. Staten, interrupts. "Why is it that every time I ask you a question, you tell me a story, instead of answering?"

I glare at her sending the coldest look possible, so she'll know I want her to back off before I lose it. Taking the time to speak now would not be productive at this juncture in the sharing experience. I stare at her hard.

"Well ok then," Dr. Staten withdraws in her seat, "never mind, I'll just chuck it up to being your process."

"It is." I roll my eyes. "Like I said, Angela and Adam are my parents. They are the best. Angela is a dentist. She recently started her own practice. Adam is a researcher. They both are hardworking, caring individuals. But no matter how many hours Adam works, my dad never misses a soccer game."

"They seem like two loving professionals."

"Yes."

"And you played soccer?" Dr. Staten asks.

"Better still, were you any good?" Timothy prods.

"Of course. I was MVP of my soccer team." I smile at Dr. Staten and roll my neck in Timothy's direction; then stare back at the empty corner.

"I didn't know that. When did you play soccer?" Dr. Staten shifts to look at me. I turn my head a smidgen to the left of her line of view.

"In High School 9th through 12th grade."

"So you were really good?" Timothy asks.

I nod yes.

"Not in college? Why did you stop?" asks Dr. Staten.

"There was no need to continue. Playtime was over. Besides, I didn't want to spoil my Dad's record."

"Oh, your Dad played soccer, too? A researcher and an athlete, huh?"

"No, he did not." I can feel myself starting to get agitated by Dr. Staten's incessant questioning about my parents.

"Then how could you spoil his record?"

"He would have missed a game!" I snapped at her. This time not playfully. I am annoyed.

"Why, Arianna?" Dr. Staten asks.

I clasp my hands, then start shaking them vigorously until my hands begin to ache. I stand up and walk to the corner of the room, I have been staring at the past fifteen minutes or so.

"Arianna, are you okay?"

"No just leave me alone!" I shout.

Dr. Staten rushes after me. "Why are you so upset?"

"I'm trying to tell you something, but you are making me sad," I whine.

"Arianna, that's a child's response."

"Is not." I whine once more. "I just wanna timeout."

"It's a child's response in a child's voice. Why?" Dr. Staten is standing behind me and I get the sense she's going to touch my shoulder.

"Don't touch me!"

"I wasn't going to Arianna."

"Liar. Leave me be!" I flinch, quickly moving my right shoulder, out of her reach.

"Talk to me, Arianna. Tell me, what's going on?" Dr. Staten asks.

I turn to look at Timothy. What he must think of me and my outbursts. He sits in his chair stoic. I guess he doesn't want to intrude on my mini tantrum. "I was a soccer player. I played in High School and I was good. I had parents, Angela and Adam. I had a home. I had love. I had it all. Then one day, I had nothing. Is that what you really want to hear?"

"Yes. Tell me, how did you go from having it all to nothing, Arianna?"

"Why are you torturing me? It already happened."

"I'm not trying to torture you."

Feeling thoroughly exposed, I tug at my shirt to wipe off my sweaty hands. I wish I had a cover, a coat, or anything to cover my face. I pull my shirt collar up over my face. "Don't look at me like that!"

"Why are you covering your face?" Dr. Staten asks.

I remain silent.

"Can you let go of your shirt?"

When I think she's about to touch me again, I instantaneously jerk my body away.

"I promise. I'm not about to touch you. I just want to understand." Dr. Staten says.

"What happened, Arianna? Tell us." Timothy calls out to me.

"Ok. Ok. Everybody just stops talking. Would you... stop standing in my space all the time!" I shriek. I cover my ears and close my eyes. "It was a rainy night! I recited the poem. I told you already. Didn't you hear what I said?"

"Yes but can you tell me in your own words?" Dr. Staten takes two steps back.

"A drunk driver. A car accident. A hospital. A life support machine, beeping like the machine beeping in the hospital the day I met you, Dr. Staten," I point at her but I don't look at either of them. "A decision has to be made. Everyone crowded around the hospital beds- still but no decision. Everyone crying, praying even cursing- but the minor- the sole survivor ultimately decides. The turning off of a life support machine. First one, then the other. No more beeping now. An orphan. Alone. Being passed around like the entrée at suppertime. A family of strangers- Aunt Maria, Uncle Paul- as welcoming as possible. Yet overwhelmed by one more mouth to feed. One more body to clothe. One more child to take care of. So of course, that leaves no time for soccer games. Pick one. Pick anyone you want." I look at Timothy, "All roads lead to what happened." I say to Dr. Staten, "Understand now?"

I blurt out my horror story in the matter of seconds.

"Such a tragedy," Dr. Staten says and takes another step backwards.

I can't move. "No, it's just *my* life." I'm glad I'm facing toward the wall so they can't see me.

"A tragic life," Timothy tries to whisper, but I hear him. Though, I pretend to ignore him.

"Arianna, how do you deal with your parents'
death? Excuse me, how did you deal with your parents' death?"

"I don't remember, Doc."

"I think you do remember Arianna?" There's urgency in Dr. Staten's tone. "Please turn around."

"I was too young."

"I know. But think back. You had some reaction to all that happened."

"Haven't I shared enough? Why isn't it *his* turn?" I point at Timothy.

"Not yet." She says calmly, "right now, I want to hear more about you. That's a lot to deal with. You must've found some way to cope?"

"Not necessarily. Things happen all the time. Let's move on."

"True they do. But we all find a way to deal with what's happened to us."

"Well, I can't remember- deal with that."

Dr. Staten ignores my contentiousness, "Some go to extreme measures to cope. While others keep it all in and hold on to it forever. Then there's the ones who lash out at other people. Which are you?"

Her words ding me. Striking both Timothy and I at the same time. She is a master in the art of delivering hard hitting words, unobtrusively - they sting, even so. Although it hurts, her flair for doing things like that is impressive.

"What did you do to deal with what happened to your parents? It's okay to tell us."

I keep quiet. I roll up my shirt sleeves to expose the healing wounds on my wrists and arms from the cutting to show to her. In the corner of my eye, I can see Timothy sit up in his chair and lean forward to see, I move my arm to show him as well. His eyes widen, and his mouth drops open wide enough for a fly to land on his tongue.

"Back then, you would cut yourself to cope?" Dr. Staten asks.

Once again, I show them, but I don't *say* anything. I am too ashamed. I lower my eyes. No one should ever be allowed to see me. I wish there was a large dark pit I could crawl into and live out the rest of my days in solace.

"It's not your fault." Dr. Staten's words pierce through the shame and hit my heart.

"What?" I need it repeated.

"It's not your fault," She says.

"Yeah," Timothy musters unconvincingly. I think he has no clue what to say but is trying in some way to be supportive.

"Arianna, cutting can be habit forming. It easily becomes a compulsive behavior — meaning that the more a person does it, the more he or she feels the need to do it. The brain starts to connect the false sense of relief from bad feelings to the act of cutting and it craves this relief the next time tension builds. You see a behavior that starts as an attempt to make you feel more in control can end up controlling you." She explains. "Hear me Arianna, this compulsive behavior can't be your fault."

Still, I say nothing. But I feel different inside. Finally, something kind of makes sense. I didn't want to slice myself repeatedly, I had to. I tried calling out for help. But the blade was easier. How does anyone control that? Just like that, my entire childhood existence is captured in the words, *it's not your fault.* What does that mean for me now? How can she help me find a better way? If I keep on doing the same thing to deal with my problem. I must be insane. How can I ever regain control- if my body reacts compulsively? Is she going to come to my house and remove all the sharp objects from my kitchen, bedroom, or purse? Cause, I'm carrying a couple paring knives in my Dolce bag, right now. I doubt it. Her fancy words are just that- fancy words. I have to live my reality. "How do you know?" I let it slip out.

"You're not the first person that I've met who cut themselves."

"Did anyone else ever get better? Or did you use fancy terms and then send them on their way?"

"What do you think?"

"I don't know, that's why I'm asking a doctor." I say it sarcastically.

"Why the sarcasm? Anyone can recover."

"That sounds like some lame stuff, you were taught to tell mentally ill people." I riposte. "I don't believe you."

"Why don't you believe me?"

"Because this is my life we're talking about. This is me right now. I'm here meeting you in this God forsaken room week after week telling you I have real problems. I have stuff going on in my life. I'm dealing with a nightmare. Then you try to reduce it to some simple psycho-babble that you probably heard at a *Psycho-Babble for Dummies* webinar."

"What's the alternative, Arianna? Cutting yourself? Or would you rather work to figure out how to cope differently? I understand you have a process but don't let your process be a crutch." Dr. Staten stands with her feet securely planted on the ground, arms at her sides like a soldier prepared to do battle. There's a boldness in her eyes when she looks into mine.

I'm running out of ways to respond. Genuinely, I am drained. I wish I could believe her. I just have a lot of doubts. My neck feels stiff. I roll my shoulders and bend my head back as far as I can. Then, I tilt my head from side to side until I hear a slight crackling sound. I just want to go home. I don't want to think about this. Plus, my legs are starting to cramp from standing in this corner.

"I don't know!" I shake my hands. "I don't want to have to decide anything right now. I just want to be left alone for a moment- please?"

"Arianna?"

"What!" I roll my eyes and yell at Timothy when I realize he's speaking.

He looks at me, the veins protruding out of his neck. I can see the annoyance as he tries his darndest not to explode or reach out and slap me into another galaxy, which he has been prone to do to women in the past.

"I mean, what," I ask again this time in a more calming tone.

"Do you feel more in control when you cut yourself?" He asks.

"Timothy," I say defensively, trying to pierce him with words, "Do you feel more in control when you slap your lady around, huh?"

"Honestly, no I don't." He answers. "I feel empty and ashamed."

Embarrassed, I look at him, "Me too."

7

GROUP SESSION

∞"I NEVER MEANT to hurt her. It's the rage inside me, like a pot on high temperature it seethes till it's too much to contain."

Dr. Staten looks at Timothy sitting in an oversized burgundy lounger, his keys, and his *Juxtapoz* magazine on the small glass table in front of him. She reaches for his magazine. "And what do you think is the source of that anger?" She asks, thumbing through the pages quickly then placing it back on the table.

"I'm not entirely sure." He grabs the magazine, sets it next to him, then sinks into the deep hollow in the middle of the lounge. His usual spot. The hollow is deep enough, nestling him in like a comfy security blanket. It's the place he goes when he wants to be detached and unreachable. "Where's the other gal who's supposed to be in here with me? Didn't you promote this as group therapy, not individual? I hope you don't plan to charge me more because that gal's not here."

"Why do you keep calling her *that gal?* You know her name Timothy."

"Because I can."

"True. But isn't it more respectful to call her by her name, instead of that gal?"

"Sure."

"You are being dismissive today, why?"

"You're putting a lot on this, Doc." Timothy exhales and nods his head. "Ok, where is Ms. Arianna? We should suffer through group together, you know. I'd rather take turns in the hot seat as you fire out questions."

"Oh is that right?"

"Yeah, for sure. You try sitting on this lounger week after week, and you let me drill you with personal question after question which seem a trifle insignificant. I bet you probably stay up all night amusing yourself with how awkward you can make us feel. Comedic skits from our life scribbled on the pages of your blue notebook, right." Timothy grits his teeth and presses the air from his tongue through his teeth. "Having someone to do the switcheroo with every once in a while, makes this bearable."

"So you like having Arianna around?"

"Now look who's being the dismissive one-"

Dr. Staten continues without acknowledging his comment, "I thought you said sharing your intimate stories with a stranger, no weak women, is weird. When did your feelings change?"

He doesn't know how to respond to her. True he had called women weak and thought it was weird to share personal stories about his childhood or striking Melissa every now and then. Somehow over the course of time- the months even- he's gotten used to being in a therapy group with women. He finds it's helpful to share experiences with Arianna and exchange battle scars as he navigates this love thing.

But if Dr. Staten is going to keep a record of everything- and at a whim use against him, perhaps it isn't best that he continues. The group sessions may prove more problematic than helpful.

"I know that look Timothy. Don't regress. Calm down now. Remember this is still a safe place."

"So you say."

"Yes it is. Why don't you feel safe?"

"I didn't say I didn't."

"Well, what's holding you back from answering my question."

"I already forgot it."

"You're being cantankerous."

"I'm allowed an off day. Right?"

"Of course. Everyone has off days. Do you think there's a root cause to everything?"

"I suppose."

"Let's try to find the root cause in this situation. Again, where does the anger come from?"

"Everywhere familiar or something."

"I don't understand. Can you elaborate?"

"You know Doc- I really can't stay long today?"

"Why is that?"

"I have a previous engagement. I decided to drop in for a quick, hello, so that gal," he looks at Dr. Staten and shrugs his shoulder, "I mean Ms. Arianna," he palms his hands in an apology, "didn't think after last session, I was being withdrawn. I didn't want her to feel like I'd treat her differently after, you know- her sharing."

"Well that's nice of you, to show such concern. I believe she'd appreciate hearing that."

"Now we'll never know because she's not here- is she?"

"No she is not. I have to give her a follow up call today. Can I tell her that you asked after her?"

"No, please don't do that. Not on my account. She probably had something more pressing like work or connecting with her man. I don't want to come in between her *process*." Timothy says using air quotes, while he speaks.

"It's interesting how you both use that term to deflect."

Timothy pokes out his lips and taps his foot on the floor, his knee bobbing up and down quickly.

"Ok." Dr. Staten says, "Since our time is going to be cut short today, how about we focus on you and not so much, Arianna? Is that ok?"

"Why? I thought you wanted me to work on my relationship with women?"

"Arianna is not one of the women in question, correct? Unless I'm missing something."

"No. I don't have a problem with Ms. Arianna." Timothy looks up and squints his eyes. "Well at least not one that I know of."

"Right. Let's talk about you and the women in your life."

"We could. For the record though, I mean for your note taking, I think Ms. Arianna is more interesting at the moment. Besides, I don't have much to say today."

"How about you explain what you mean by *everywhere familiar* or *something* in more detail? How does familiarity or something trigger your rage? Do you mean everything makes you angry?"

"No, I meant what I said," Timothy snaps.

"There's that cantankerousness again." Dr. Staten folds her hands in her lap, "As always, I'm just trying to understand."

"Don't try to pacify me like I'm a child or something." He says sharply.

"I'm not. I just want you to know I'm only here to try to understand. I'm not trying to tell you what to do, how to feel or how to act? You have a choice in this. My role is to help you think through other options before you react. Isn't that what you asked of me when we first met?"

Timothy sits silently, contemplating.

Dr. Staten waits patiently during the silence.

"I can be in a new environment and suddenly be reminded of a familiar setting from my childhood." Timothy slinks into the crevice of his seat and stares at the ground. "It's like when I'm in this unfamiliar place and it reminds me of something bad, I get angry. Really angry."

He glares toward her direction.

"Even now, there are certain parts of my new spot that remind me of that house I used to live in with *that woman* and *her husband.* Then Melissa goes and stands in the exact spot- that bad memory spot which causes me to react in an unfavorable way, if you know what I mean." He bobs his head from side to side looking down. "Or she'll do or say something *that woman* did or said before," he bangs his fist against his head, "I can't stop the memories of *that woman* and *her husband.* I get enraged. It's consuming. It's... everything familiar.... or just something."

"So by that woman and her husband, you mean your Mother and Father?" Dr. Staten asks.

"Yep, you sure are a sharp one Doc. There's nothing getting pass you today." He says snidely.

"Then you get angry."

"Enraged!"

"In that... familiar moment... it's no longer about you and Melissa. Instead you're reacting like your father did *toward* your mother?"

He bounces up then down on the lounger to deepen the hollow in the cushion. He clenched his hands, rubbing them fervently till

74

tiny ashy flakes of dry skin shed off them and they turned a reddish-purple color against his dark skin.

"It's okay Timothy." Dr. Staten smiles at him. "Let's figure this out together."

"Is it time to go?" He asks gruffly. "Is this session over?"

"Are you ready to go?"

"I told you before I... I... I have a previous engagement." Timothy stammers his words as he stands up. He grabs his magazine, sunglasses, and coat.

"Timothy," She touches the sleeve of his coat, "if you keep leaving as soon as the conversation gets uncomfortable, you'll miss an opportunity for a breakthrough. Is that really what you want?"

"Are you telling me the session isn't over and I need to stay?" He tugs his coat sleeve out of her grip.

"No I'm not." Dr. Staten folds her hands in her lap. "I only want you to be here as long as you want to be. Like I said before, you have a choice in this. It's your journey to a healthy place."

"Well I told you when I arrived, I couldn't stay long."

"Yes you did."

"I was being truthful when I said I have tons of important things on my schedule, you know?"

"I realize that."

"So what do you want from me, Doc?"

"How's Melissa?"

"Who?" He squawks at her question.

"Melissa." She asks, steadying her body toward his. "You haven't really spoken of her or the two of you in a while. Not since before Arianna joined us."

"Remember the familiar spot I said Melissa stood in and I got enraged?"

"Yes."

"Well in that moment a while ago, when I was so furious at something Melissa said or did that reminded me of that *woman*. I took the back of my hand and whipped it across her face three times. Whipping it until my hand bled. Actually it was the red from her pulsating bloody nose that dripped through my fingers and down my knuckles." Timothy stares at the back of his hands and wipes them on the sides of his jeans. "She left soon after that. She said she couldn't take being someone's rag doll anymore. Being shaken, tossed aside or dragged on the ground- trailing behind someone one minute then lavished on the next. So, she left."

"Did you-"

"Go after her?" Timothy looks up at Dr. Staten who's intently eyeing his mouth like his words are more important than the air she breathes. "No. What good would it do? I don't even blame her. It does however make me more confused about *that woman*. Melissa left me after six months. She got fed up and high tailed it out of my life. Why did *that woman* stay thirty years? Why didn't she leave him? He wasn't even trying to get better." The tone of his voice is muted and his now sunken body feels empty.

"And now you have to leave. So it continues." Dr. Staten lowers her voice to match Timothy's. Her words still ring out like the hour chime on a grand clock tower. "Sounds like there's still work you need to face head on in here, to make you better out there. There are better choices."

"You know- I really wish Arianna were here to ease the blow of your words!" He shakes his head from side to side. "I can't. Not today." He pops up from the chair again, grabs his keys and magazine then hurries out of the room. "Later doc." He calls back out of habit.

8

GROUP SESSION

∞"WHY IS IT so hot in here? Was it this hot last session? The one I missed?" I take an envelope out of my purse and fan it back-and-forth in front of my face. "Whew!"

"I know right?" Timothy says while mindlessly rummaging through his man bag, searching for something with the girth with which to fan himself. He decides on his magazine, Juxtapoz- or as he calls it 'the go to read for artists and sculptors' but the hefty periodical slips from his fingers, banging against his knee before landing on the floor in front of him. "Ouch.... this monstrosity hit my funny bone!" Timothy yells at me.

I laugh at his pain, which immediately makes me wonder if automatically laughing when someone gets hurt is normal.

I'm probably supposed to be more compassionate. Or am I being my usual overthinking, over-processing self. "Seriously Dr. Staten, why is it so hot in here? I mean it's excruciatingly hot? This is like... an unbearable heat." I fan the envelope faster. "I know there's a heatwave outside but I was hoping not to stroke out in therapy. A meeting room should at least be cool."

Dr. Staten ignores me.

"What, is the central air system broken too, like me? Did somebody forget to turn the fans on or pay the bill? It's a church for heaven sake! You would think the temple of God would be cooler. You know because of heaven and all- and not the other place. But it's hot as hell fire in here!"

I watch Dr. Staten walk over to the wall unit. Tapping the face of the thermostat repeatedly, making a weird- Bop, Bop da bop, rhythm a couple of times. Beep, beep, beep accompanies every finger tap in a loud hypnotic tone. It reminds me of the incessant noise of the IV machine, the day I met her at the hospital.

"Okay. Enough. That should do it!" I yell. "What's with all the beeping?" She is quiet. Dr. Staten's gotten use to my mini outbursts and now is oblivious to my sporadic tantrums. She continues trying to manipulate the central air monitor. I wonder if her silence is triggered by annoyance. It was her idea, after all, for me to be more expressive in this 'safe space'- as she calls it. Constantly asking me, how are you feeling or want to share? Today is the day she chooses to be silent. Not cool.

"So what, you have no response for me?" I ask it brashly in a disapproving tone. I want her to know, at this moment I am feeling anything but safe. "Why are people always doing this to me? Every time. Why does the same thing keep happening to me?"

I want an answer because my question deserves an explanation. What I really want to say is like Denzel Washington said in that movie Philadelphia, "Explain it to me like I'm a four-year-old." But, those words don't come out. I just huff, lean back in my seat and wait.

"People aren't doing things to you, Arianna." Dr. Staten says. When the cool air bustles on with a low sputtering sound she smiles, nods her head and exhales in triumph. "You are doing it to yourself."

Now I'm the one who's silent. I am seriously agitated. That's not the response I wanted. She could have just kept that comment to herself.

"I can help you take control, if you want." Dr. Staten says.

"Well that man who's married to my mother, did this to me." Timothy interjects, finally.

"No he didn't, Timothy." She turns and looks at Timothy. "You did this to yourself as well. Depriving yourself. Punishing yourself. Mimicking him. You did those things. While he went ahead with his life. You tortured yourself." She speaks to both Timothy and I, "And no amount of group sessions- sitting in excruciatingly hot rooms- are going to change what happened. Right now you both are faced with a choice. Be a part of making the change you want to see or stay alone." She pauses.

I look over at Timothy who is fuming through his scrunched up nostrils. I can feel the fumes coming through his nose. He sits there like one of those cartoon characters darting back and forth about to explode. I guess he's inwardly contemplating whether to slap her like he slaps the Melissa chic he dates. But I doubt he'd ever do that. He does too. That's why with each fleeting moment, he's growing calmer, and the fuming nostrils ease to a simple inhale and exhale.

"Perhaps your life didn't turn out the way you thought it would. Or it's a mere glimpse of what you imagined. Embrace it. Recreate what you become, starting today. Be afraid--not paralyzed by your past."

"How am I," for a moment I forget Timothy's sitting a stones' throw away from me. "I mean- we do this?" I ask it secretly, praying to hear something useful.

"Let's give Brian," Dr. Staten nods at Timothy, "or your parent's even, time to think what they think or feel how they feel. While Timothy works on Timothy and Arianna works on Arianna. And if in the meantime you all are less than perfect, so what. Just keep moving forward Walt Disney Aires." She smiles at us.

"Walt Disney Aires?" I say.

"Yeah you know, Walt Disney's coined phrase- keep moving forward." Timothy cocks his head to the side and puckers his lips to send me an air kiss.

I roll my eyes and neck at him.

"Correct." Dr. Staten gasps. Neither of us expected for him to know that. "Now back to you two. Try not to turn your slips into falls." She ends in her usual serious tone I've become accustomed to.

"Well I guess you told us," I say to Dr. Staten.

Sweet, sensitive, kind-eyed Dr. Staten with her soft hands and her 'free to be your best you' attitude, just, told us in not some many words-- to grow the hell up and to move on! Or that's what I gathered from her commentary. From the look of Timothy, who's no longer scowling at her- but instead nodding his head profusely; agrees with me. Don't turn your slips into falls. Her final words sound in my ears, repeatedly. Maybe, it's time to tell her what happened? I think. Next, session. My scarier more cautious inner self responds.

9

GROUP SESSION

∞AT OUR NEXT session, I share the story of the dreadful night:

I sit on the edge of my bed, staring into the abyss that is now my world. Arms' dangling, body thin, face a pale brown- the emptiness engulfs the room and makes itself a dwelling place. I try to get my mind and body to do something.... anything, but I don't move. So, I try to focus on a better time. But, the emptiness is too powerful. I'm still for what seems like hours trying to make myself aware of the surroundings. I command my mind, body and soul even to focus. I know I need to be what I fear- be stronger. Starting with my foot, since it's the furthest point from my biggest problem area, my mind, I tell it to slide out straight. For two reasons, one, to reposition my leg because paresthesia has set in and two, it seems like a simple thing to do.

My brain sends a message to my foot to slide across the ground and lay straight; first the left foot and then the right foot follow suit. I slide my hips, waist, chest, arms, neck, and head all little to the left till I am in a new position. Now for the hard part. I tell my mind to focus on the room. Eyes see. Stop staring blankly. I look around the room. Everything goes from blurry to bright in minutes. I finally start to get my bearings. I am in my room, sitting on the edge of my bed in my nightgown. The room is a shambles, as if it's been hit by Hurricane Katrina, or Hurricane Sandy. Clothes, shoes, and papers lay in clumps across the floor with globs of red spots on different articles- like patches on a quilt, litter my bedroom floor.

A night stand is toppled over and pieces of cracked glass bulbs are at my feet. Next to it, my linen curtains are hanging off the separated bent rod and damaged pane. They dangle toward the ground swaying every time a breeze blows in through the window. It's cold and wet here. I feel numb, which I surmise has something to do with my arms. The lower part of my left and right arms are numb. There's six cuts on my wrists. The blood continues to slide down my wrist through my hands and onto my bed. I can feel my pressure lowering. And I realize the red spots on the littered piles are mine. There are traces of me stained throughout my room.

The cuts burn but I feel an awkward pleasure in the burning. Somehow, it masks the overwhelming hurt. In my right hand, there is a thick bloody blade.

∞∞∞∞

"What happened to you?" There's another person in the room with me.

"What do you mean?" I ask.

"How did you get like this? This isn't you?" I can tell the unusually harsh voice is Brian's.

I don't know how to answer his question, or at least not with something that makes sense. So, I remain silent for a long time.

"Yes it is."

"Not true. When we met you were confident. Strong. That's the sexy woman I remember." He says.

"See that's where you're wrong. That person doesn't exist. She's a myth concocted to keep you interested."

"No Arianna... no one can pretend that long." I hear the pain in his voice through each word.

I should feel empathy for him. I can't concentrate on that part of me now. "I did."

"Well then I guess the jokes on me. You fooled me into loving a fake you."

"Wrong again sweetie, you could never love me because you never knew me." I lie to him hoping he'll walk out, quickly, and abandon me like everyone else I've loved. I don't have the strength to keep up the charade.

"Bye Arianna. Or whoever you are." He walks out the bedroom. My front door squeals open then slams shut.

That's what brings me to the point of sitting alone in the empty bloody room. When the blade first got in my hand, I forget. What day is it? I have no idea. I look down at my blood stained satin sheets. Were they ruined? Probably. But, I really didn't care. How did my skin get sliced up like someone's been dicing carrots with one of those multipurpose kitchen dicers from the home shopping network? No recollection. But did I feel an ounce of pleasure, in the coldness of my skin, the wetness of the blood, the piercing of the blade or the burning cut- absolutely. Unquestionably, yes! It is like, the blade opening my skin is me opening my mouth and finally *YELLING!*

∞∞∞

Now, I look up at Dr. Staten and over to Timothy both sitting there in what I determine as awe. "Brian thought he knew me. I don't even know me. There is a constant war going on inside me between the person I am and the woman I want to be." I pause for questions. There's just silence. Perhaps they're in shock.

Timothy has an *"I knew she was crazy"* look on his face- though he tries to hide it with a whimsical smile every few seconds which make him look like a man with a nervous twitch. While, Dr. Staten gives me a simple nod.

"Seriously. I don't understand half the things I do. Brian had a good heart. The moment I figured that out I knew what I had to do."

"What was that?" Dr. Staten asks.

"I knew I had to get rid of him. A good heart and a damaged woman—don't mix."

"You enjoyed being around him right, Arianna?" She asks.

"Yes. He made me laugh... and smile ... and feel safe. He was handsome. Charismatic. A real charmer. He always seemed genuine. In the beginning it was better," I pause. "Honestly, the entire time we were together was pretty great. I was just waiting."

"Waiting for what?" She asks.

"For him to leave."

"For him to leave?"

"If you're going to keep repeating me. This session is going to take double the time." I snarl at her.

"I'm not trying to agitate you, Arianna."

"I'm not agitated." I lie. "I just want to get through this so I can get out of the hot seat."

"You're not in the hot seat."

"Feels pretty heated to me."

"If I try to limit my interruptions, would that help?"

"Yes. Whatever." I say.

"Ok. Go on. You were talking about waiting *for him to leave.*"

"Right. The waiting turned into stress or wondering which day he'd l...leave." I stutter at the word leave. That word hurts to let out more than any other word. "Then it became pretending to be someone else to make him stay. Pretension equals exhaustion. While I was pretend laughing- at every joke or pretend to smile to mask how I really felt, I started bleeding to death inside. I needed some relief. Something real. Cutting was my vice of choice. A way to let my insides out."

"Why do you think you were bleeding inside?"

"Because when I met Brian, I thought maybe this guy is as damaged as me. Maybe there's a chance. No way, he'd ever leave because he's just like me. Then I got to know him and it became obvious. He was not damaged. He just had some baggage. Like all the other normal people walking around in this world. A little baggage does not match up against damage. Baggage can't handle damage. You can't compare the two. Baggage wouldn't survive"

Dr. Staten leans in close to me like we are the only two people in the room, "But baggage is not perfect either. We all have things that make us imperfect. We are all struggling to survive"

"Then why did I end up here alone and not Brian?"

"Perhaps he would be here. If you'd let him in, Arianna."

"Perhaps?"

"Yes, perhaps."

"You know even after all I had said and done. He still sent a text."

"What did he have to say?"

"Nothing much." I purse my lips. "Actually I keep it in my phone. I can't erase it." I grab my phone from my Coach bag. "He texts, *I want to get to know the real you. Is it too late?*"

"Did you respond?" Timothy asks. He's been so quiet, I forget he's even here.

"Yes."

"Well?"

"I wanted to respond with something intoxicating to entice him to come back home. Like: my love it's not too late. Let's start over. But my actual reply, *I suffered in silence, you used your voice! You're always giving me what you think I want but never giving me what I need to receive!*"

I huff. "That crap of lies was our final text exchange."

"What does that even mean?" Timothy squints his eyes at me.

"I don't know," I shrug my shoulders. "Who cares anyway?"

"Well," Dr. Staten looks at me and Timothy, "here's where we figure it all out, together. What does a healthy relationship look and feel like? How do you get there? Both of you have unresolved issues with loved ones. It's those unresolved issues that are making it difficult for you to live a full life. You both have been going along through life every day, in and out of relationships that in your mind-resemble love. It's not. It's dishonest. Your fears control your interactions. In order to get to a healthy place, you have to be honest with yourself about the true source of your problems, and confront it." She leans back in her chair and looks at Timothy. "You have to deal with the hurt or betrayal from your parents." She turns toward me, "or in your case- the loss of your parents."

"I don't know if I'm ready?" I admit shyly.

"Yes you are." She says dismissively.

"How do you know? I just said, ``I didn't even know."

"Do you like the way you are now?"

"No"

89

"Do you want to get to a better place?"

"Of course, I do."

"Do you think if you go it alone, you'll stop cutting yourself?"

"Whoa, that's a low blow, doc." Timothy says.

Dr. Staten shoots him a look that obviously translates into *being quiet now*. Which he does. "Arianna, do you think if you do this- in your time- you'll stop cutting yourself?"

"Doubt it." I understand her question. She's not trying to be crude- only wants me to know it's time for honest self-reflection.

"Do you trust that I sincerely want to help you get to a healthier place?"

"I guess."

"No more guessing," Dr. Staten sits up in her chair. "I'm asking do you trust that my helping you is sincere?"

"Yes!" I bellow, so she understands I believe she cares.

"Well then trust me when I say, you are ready." Dr. Staten leans back in her chair. "As part of the process I want you both to take a huge leap of faith to make amends with your loved ones. Any way you choose. Whether it's an impromptu meet up, a letter, a phone call, even a homing pigeon will suffice. Timothy, your assignment is your parents. And Arianna," she looks at me intensely, "Brian is your assignment. Try to extend a figurative, olive branch. Meet with them. Open up by revisiting the past. Express to them, how it affects how you relate to the world and everyone in it. Transparency is what I'm asking here."

"Well my mother has been inquiring as to my next visit. I guess I can make *one* family dinner. No guarantees." Timothy says indifferently.

"Good first step," Dr. Staten smiles at him, "Please try to muster a little more enthusiasm."

"I've been avoiding Brian for months now," I say. "Maybe, now's the time for us to reconnect."

"Good Arianna. Be honest with him."

"What should I say?"

"Anything. It doesn't have to be scripted. Just talk to him. Tell him about your Adam and Angela, like you told us."

"How will that help? They're not even here anymore? I mean, they're not even alive."

Dr. Staten's eyes widen, and she begins to smile. "That's right, Arianna. Your parents are not alive. You may not realize it right now, but being able to acknowledge that, is huge. Tell Brian about them."

"I think my story will scare him away and make him more apprehensive. That's a lot to lay on him."

"How do you know?"

"Why would I chance it?"

"Because he's asking you to let him in. He's asking you to take a chance. What did he say in that text he sent you?"

"Which one?"

"You know which one. What did he say? What did he ask you?"

"He said he wanted to get to know the real me. Then he asked if it was too late?"

"Exactly! That's someone who is imploring you to let them in. Isn't he worth a chance?"

Thunderously, my heart pounds, I grab my chest to stop the impending panic attack. I quickly move my hands from my chest which begin to shake frantically from side to side- till my wrists hurt. I will myself to stop. Powerless, I shove my hands in my pockets to hide the nervousness. *Calm down and breathe.* I say inwardly, and I do. Then, I smile. *See girl, you're fine- keep breathing?* I am not positive I can do this. But I have just committed to try.

"Yes, he is." I say

10

TIMOTHY, There's a MAN in the MIRROR?

∞"HELLO?" TIMOTHY CALLS pushing the screen door wide open. "Anyone home?" He releases the screen that smacks against the outer door panel.

He walks inside the small red brick framed house he grew up in. It still holds an old musty smell like damp clothes that were left out too long and didn't have time to properly dry. Nothing has changed. The darkness causes him to feel a lingering amount of lassitude when he walks through every orifice of the house; advisedly the direct opposite to his house. The muggy hallway makes the house suffocatingly hot. He tugs at his shirt collar a couple of times to pluck off the beads of perspiration and let the cool breeze skim across his chest.

"Mother, I'm here." He calls. "It's Timothy. Your only son, remember."

An older woman in a nice fitting floral dress appears at the end of the long shotgun hallway. She has a slim frame, which he thinks is a little too petite and fragile looking but it's evident from her toned body, warm amber skin and bone structure that she would be pretty by anyone's standard. Although her dress falls against her gracefully fitted, it still looks weathered. "Timothy dear. I'm so pleased to see you." She reaches for him, "come and give your mother a hug. You know it has been almost three years since you've been home."

"Not home, Mother. It's been years since I have been in your house." He says.

"Semantics dear." She smiles at him. "Please don't get testy already. You just arrived. Come and give me a hug." She grabs him, pulls him close to her skeletal frame and inhales quietly. "You always have the best scent. What cologne do you wear? Are you hungry?

Thirsty? I can get something for you. Sit down. Stay awhile." The swift words spew out her mouth. She points toward a small light blue cloth loveseat.

"I doubt its cologne more like the soap I use. I ate earlier. So, I'm not hungry. Nor thirsty. But thanks for asking. I'm fine. I can't stay long. I just wanted to come by to check in to see how you were doing." Timothy tries to recollect her questions in order. "I think I answered everything."

"Oh nonsense." She tugs at his jacket dismissively. "Please don't tell me that you traveled over an hour from Princeton for a five-minute visit? Surely you can stand to be with your family longer than that, Timothy." She huffs. "Now give me your jacket and sit down. I'll go get your father. He's been eager to see you; counting the days since we last spoke.

"Now who's being dramatic, mother? Counting the days... really? I seriously doubt he has been sober enough to function, much less to count."

"Timothy, honestly." She snaps. "Sit down and be cordial."

"Of course, mother." He says sarcastically. "Since when have I ever been anything less than cordial?"

"A minute ago. So there," she says jokingly.

Timothy laughs unexpectedly at her quick wit.

"What, a smile? There's my son." She smiles at him.

"Please, mother?" Timothy's smile widens showing most of his brilliant white teeth and left dimple. He's surprised when he notices his breathing is steady and there are no knots in his stomach. He's been in his mother's presence for more than five minutes and he is content.

When she motions again for him to sit down, he gives her his jacket and slowly eases down onto the couch.

"See Timothy, that wasn't too difficult. Was it?"

"So far so good." He says.

"Would you like a glass of water?"

"Yes, a glass of water would be perfect. I am feeling a little parched." He says raising the left corner of his mouth to smirk. He feels himself trying to be more agreeable and figures while he's there, he will make an effort. If, for nothing else- at least, he can tell Dr. Staten, he did his part. He was obliging.

"Great, I will get you a nice cold glass of water. This house is extremely muggy." She passes him a piece of tissue from the box on the end table next to him." Here, you're sweating. I do apologize, dear." She says; then heads down the long hallway toward the kitchen at the back of the house.

"Thanks, mother." He calls.

She stops midway down the hall and pauses for a moment. Then, she turns to look at him, gives a short nod, blinks her eyes and smiles again. She quickly disappears through the kitchen door. He wonders if the way she looks at him is because of his "*Thanks*" or at his calling her "*Mother*" unpretentiously. Either way, he is glad she seems pleased.

He scans the living room, next to the light blue sofa and matching loveseat is an aged round oak end table that's been painted white. It has an antique brass lamp, and an old photo encased in glass with a metal frame. It is a photo of him and his two sisters. He shakes his head as he slides his fingers across the oak table. *Why would anyone paint over such classic hardwood?* He shakes his head again when he grabs the framed photo.

The metal picture frame is rusting and the glass is so dusty with a finger- he etches the letters **T I M** then in one swoop wipes it away. A cloud of dust swirls off the frame and up into the air. He cleanses the glass using the tip of tissue his mother gave him to have a better view of the image. He stares at the three familiar faces of him and his two younger sisters, Jocelyn and Jacklyn, smiling back at him. The three are sitting outside of the house on the front steps. The red brick pops out in the background of the photo. It seems brighter, cleaner and definitely less muggy in the glossy finish than it is now.

He brings the photo closer to his eyes, squinting to see the three little outfits. He is wearing a black and white pinstripe short suit, a pair of black dress socks almost up to his knees, and a pair of fancy black patent leather shoes. His two sisters are wearing matching pink dresses, overlain with white lace netting, which has puffy pink and yellow flowers draped along the hem. They also wear fancy white shoes with black soles. The girls sit on the first step facing one another, arms folded in their laps, legs crossed at the ankle, smiling. Timothy sits on the higher third step off to the left side of his sisters. His elbows on his knees propping up his smiling face. His huge smile can't disguise his two missing front teeth. He shakes his head and laughs at his younger, awkwardly looking innocent but happy self.

"Do you remember that day?" His mother asks, reaching out to hand him the glass of water and napkin. "Please, use the coaster?" She points to a wooden coaster on the end table.

"Excuse me... I didn't hear you coming." Timothy takes the glass and places it on the coaster before sipping it. "No, I do not recall that day at all. When was this? How old was I?"

"Let's see," she looks up toward the ceiling, "you had to be around six." His mother pauses, puts her hand on her chin as if in deep thought. "Yes you were six. Your father and I were taking the three of you to Easter service. Yancy loved to get you all dressed up so he could parade you around the church like movie stars. You know, your father was the photographer? That's where you get your creative artistic flair." She says.

"Wish it was the only thing I inherited." Timothy mumbles.

"I was still in the house getting ready." She rambles on. "He was always the quicker dresser. He would get up early Sunday morning to get dressed then get you children ready. It always took me longer. So your father would pass the time by having you all take pictures in front of the house. He has albums full of pictures of the three of you."

"Are you sure? I don't remember any of this?"

"Yes, I may be aging but my memory is still pretty sharp." She says. "Your father was not all bad, Timothy. How proud he was of you children, from the moment we'd enter the front hall of the church, he'd stop to introduce you to everyone. His kids didn't even think to mention me at all. He'd talk endlessly about each of your achievements, as if you were a famous scholar or Nobel Peace Prize winner. Every good grade. Every award was pronounced. Every weird thing you do at home. He had a story for it. He couldn't help himself."

"Well that's not what I remember about my childhood."

"I know. You only remember the bad things. He's the most unbearable deplorable monster in your eyes. Who never did anything nice for you? Cruel, right?"

"Yes, that's exactly how I remember it." He places the picture back on the end table and pushes it out of view. "I'm guessing the photos of him beating us didn't make it onto the mantel, end table or photo albums of the great photographer, huh?"

"Timothy please. He wasn't himself. He had an actual sickness. He was an alcoholic. Can you try to understand what he went through? Alcoholism is a terrible disease for anyone to endure."

Timothy rises from the couch and paces silently back and forth in the small living space. His heart pumps quicker. He massages his chest, rubbing it in a circular motion to calm himself and steady his heart rate. He stops pacing, then flops back onto the sofa. "Are you serious?" He says throwing his hands into the air. "That's all you can say to explain to him?" *Why can't she just admit his father was a lousy drunk who cared more about drinking or abusing her than getting help for his disease?* "Why do you always defend him?"

"I'm not, dear. I'm just trying to explain."

"No." He raises his voice. "You are trying to justify his mistreatment of you....me....all of us! Why can't you just admit, what he did to us was cruel and unwarranted?" Timothy sits up in his chair and glares at his mother. "He doesn't get a pass because when I was six, he took pictures of me, Joce and Jackie."

"Timothy, I' m not."

"Or that he paraded us around at church. Did he parade us around after he beat us too? Did he captivate everyone with stories of beating you? Isn't that a major accomplishment? That we survived being terrorized by him?"

"This was before he started drinking. He's a goo---."

"Please don't say good man! I'd rather we look at the old pictures than you utter those lies." Timothy shakes his head. "No, he's not a good man. He's never been a good man. What he is...is a loud-mouthed bully and drunken coward! I don't see that being displayed. Why is it that there's only one picture of this fictitious happy family?" He points at the picture. "If he were... ah as you say... a "good man"... shouldn't we have a plethora of happy childhood snapshots around the house? Why is there only one photo? One dusty, frame rusted photo of the good man and his children?"

"Timothy, I can see you are working yourself up into a frenzy over this." She places her hand on his shoulder. "Calm down, dear." She rubbed his arm and whispered. "Calm down please or you'll wake up your father."

He brushes her hand away. "Calm down or I'll wake him up. He really is all you care about, huh?" He gets up. "May I have my coat? I knew this was a bad idea."

"But, Timothy you've only been here a little while."

"What does it matter anyway?" He shrugs his shoulders. "He's still asleep. I thought you said he was so excited to see me. He was counting the days till my arrival for our enjoyable family dinner. I guess excitable people go comatose to contain their enthusiasm." Timothy scoffs at her. "Unless he's been drinking. Was he drinking, Priscilla?"

"Timothy, oh, Timothy." Her tone, timorous.

"Repeating my name, over and over again is not an appropriate response. Was he drinking, Priscilla?"

"You no longer refer to me as Mother?"

"Answer the question."

"No, that is not it. He had to work late last night, so he took a nap so he would be more-"

"No need to explain. Will you please, just get my coat?"

"Dear you didn't even drink your glass of water," she points to the glass of water with melted ice cubes floating on the surface, the sweat dripping off the side of the glass and onto the wooden coaster.

"I'm not thirsty."

"You said you were."

"Fine." Timothy grabs the glass and gulps the water down. "Are you satisfied? Now, will you please bring me my coat?" He gets up from the couch and starts down the long hallway toward the back rooms. "Or just tell me which room closet you put it in and I will get it, myself!"

"Prissy, who's there? Whass all that yellin' bout?" Timothy hears his father calling from one of the back rooms. "Is that, him? Is that my boy?"

100

"Yes, Yancy," she calls back. "Please Timothy." She squeezes his arm gently and whispers. "Stay. He's up now and you're already here. He'll want to see you. He won't understand if you leave now."

"Will you just get my coat? He's a good man, remember. Good men are very understanding." He says with an air of sarcasm.

"We were having fun, weren't we? Let's not spoil everything now because of something that happened years ago." She pleads. "Make new memories starting today, and let go of the past."

"You don't understand, do you?" Timothy says. "I can't make new memories until I deal with the past. The one thing you refuse to acknowledge or much less- deal with. I can't keep playing pretend with you and Yancy! Living a lie is not helping anyone." His mother looks up at him, turns to walk away.

"Now, where are you going?" he shrieks.

"I'm going to get your coat, as requested." She says walking down the hall and into one of the side bedrooms.

Timothy walks toward the front door. He hears a series of footsteps and doors opening and closing. He is praying his mother comes back with his coat, fast. *It's time to go,* he murmured. He's too angry to confront his father now. Acknowledging his father's existence is nowhere near the top of his to-do list right now.

Timothy hears muffled sounds coming from the back bedroom, as if whispers between lovers. But he knows there's no love in this house. The door creaks as it opens followed by a series of footsteps. He lowers his head slowly toward the ground. Immediately, his body halts. He's immobile. The footsteps grow louder and quicker. They sound too heavy to be his mother. He can feel someone approaching him. But I can't look up. "Oh God, let me be wrong. Let it be my mother and not her husband?" He whispers.

"Tim, uhm Tim, Son, why you standin' at the door? You not stayin' for dinner- eh?" Timothy's father calls. "Whass' wrong with you? Look at me."

Timothy raises his head slowly at his father's command. All his abilities recovered in an instant. He can move. "I'm fine. I have to go. I have some outstanding projects. Besides, I've lost my appetite."

"You know how long ya' mom slaved over that stove, all so we could eat dinner together?"

"Well I can't make myself hungry, when I'm not. Nor, can you force feed me." Timothy smirks. "Oh wait, you know all too well about force feeding someone. If memory serves me correctly, that's what you used to do to my mother, right?"

"Nope. I don't know what you talkin' bout."

"Of course you don't. That's exactly why I'm going to put on my coat, walk out your front door and go home."

"You is home, boy." The base in his father's voice intensifies with each word. "Why, you... too... good... to call this here home?"

"This house was never a home. You made sure of that. If you and my mother choose to live in denial with how you raised us-- I can't stop you. I will not condone or excuse your ill treatment toward my Mother, Joce, Jackie, or me."

"Oh that's what you come here for. To talk down to me and blame all the bad things on me. It's like you think you was a perfect, child! Well you weren't." Timothy's father walks over to him. "I can only remember you listenin' and doing right as a small boy. When you got older and started smellin' yourself- you ain't listen to me no more. I expected Prissy to keep you all in line. You and the girls."

"What?" Timothy rushes toward his father to meet him in the middle of the hallway. "We were not out of line! You were just a lousy contemptible drunk, who slapped his wife around for the hell of it like a coward. And when anyone came to her aid or tried to stop you, namely me, you would strike, punch or kick them." Timothy sucks his teeth. "I wasn't smellin' myself as you put it. You were the smelly one, Yancy. The pungent, alcohol-ridden drunk!" His eyes examined his father from head to toe. "That's why I'm refusing to have dinner with either of you. That's why I have no appetite. Could you blame me, really? Coming here was a huge mistake."

"Ya' got that right! Cuz, you don't come into my home and tell me how to run my family!" His father shouts; then takes a big gulp of the clear looking ice cubed drink in his hand.

Timothy hadn't noticed the glass in his father's hand before. "Family. You were never sober enough to father a family. And this," he points around, "was never a family. You were too busy drinking....not water." He looks at the glass, then back up at his father.

"Just because you had successes- don't make you better than me. Callin' me Yancy and yellin' at me. Or callin' ya Mom, Priscilla. Who do you think you are, boy?"

Timothy's mother rushes down the hall toward them. He could hear her brisk footsteps. He doesn't acknowledge her. All his focus stays on the big balding man standing in front of him. They are now face to face and almost chest to chest. For Timothy, he and the man he's the spitting image of are the only two that exist- the man he refuses to call Father.

"I'm not going to take much more disrespect, ya' hear?" Yancy barks.

Timothy takes a step back. His feet securely planted on the ground and hands balled into a fist at his side. He readies his stance in case this spirited discussion turns physical.

"Ti.. Timothy, here's your coat." His mother stutters, stretching the coat toward him. "Everyone calm down. Timothy, you know your father-"

"Not now, mother, please." Timothy responds with his back to her cutting her off mid-sentence. "I'm just having a conversation with your good husband- on his role as father and head of the house."

"Just give him an opportunity to speak, Tim. He's been waiting a long time to reconcile with you. That is not an easy thing to do. He knew you would be apprehensive."

"What? Are you trying to find a way to defend this?" Timothy points at his Father. "Why do you let him treat you like trash? Treat us like this. While you stand there looking feeble and pathetic?"

"Tim, dear, I'm just trying—"

"Hey there, you don't talk to my wife like that!" His father, cautions. His large bug-like eyes widen with each inflection off his voice.

"Wife? No sir, not your wife! You mean more like your whipping post or doormat. You just want someone to control. Someone subservient to cover up your sorry excuse for a life, isn't that more accurate?"

His father stumbles toward him. Timothy shifted his position to a defensive position. His body shivers, as if frigid from a cold breeze. But there was no breeze, only a demon of the abused child reverberated in him, coming out bustling. Then, he saw his alcoholic dad driven by the disease rushing toward him.

"Back up dad, before I lay you out." Timothy quickly warns while rocking his body side to side.

"Well at' lease you know my name. That's right boy. I'm still your dad." He slurs stumbling closer to Timothy.

"Yancy!" His mother cries. "Please stop it and back away from our son."

His father glares at her. Then, he brushes her away with a wave of his glass, spilling most of its contents onto the floor. "See what you made me do, Prissy? Let me be woman. I need to settle this with the boy."

"Yes Yancy. I think you should listen to your wife and back up!" Timothy repeats. His fists balled, body swaying and arms stiffen until the frame of his muscles show through his pin striped dress shirt.

"Timothy dear," his mother rests her hand on his back, "why don't you go home now and come back another day? Like you said, you really don't have an appetite." She speaks quickly. Her voice quivers.

He doesn't move an inch even at her touch. "Why do you stay? You can go anywhere. Live anywhere. Moreover, why would you stay here, take this or want to live like this?" He shakes his body to relax himself. "I can't deal with this right now. I only have a couple of months before my exhibition." He shakes his head. "This was a bad idea. I'm out!" He says, grabbing his coat and storming toward the door.

"Good get outta here. Who needs ya? Just get before I," His father slurs.

Timothy whips his body around and scowls at his father. He scans his father's shriveling body and limp hand trying to grip the half emptied glass- of what he presumes is alcohol- and smirks. "Before you do what? You may still beat on her but look at me, I am a grown man! The only reason I spared you is because I am determined not to be you. Never to become this image I see staring back at me every time I look in the mirror. I am determined to be a better man, husband, and one day father-- than you ever were."

104

"Then maybe instead of complainin' all the time about what I did or didn't do. You should thank me!" His father, taunts.

"Yancy please," Timothy's mother says "leave him alone."

"Shut up, Prissy ain't nobody talkin' to you. Don't make me more upset!" His father lifts his glass and waves it in her direction.

"Priscilla, you stay here with this belligerent ingrate, for what?" Timothy asks.

"What do you want from me, Timothy?" She asks.

"I want you to tell the truth. Be honest- for once."

"He's my husband."

"And you need a new line."

"But-"

"Like I said, I have to get ready for my exhibition. Goodbye Priscilla." Timothy walks down the hall. "Go back to sleep, Yancy. I don't have any more time to spend on you." The screen door slams behind him.

11

ARIANNA, PLEASE!

∞**I DON'T UNDERSTAND** why Dr. Staten's assignment makes me feel uncomfortable. I stay up the whole night tossing and turning in the bed contemplating all the ways this idea can turn out badly. Every outcome is the same. Disaster. All, from following her directions to see Brian. *There's no way I can survive this.*

I try sleeping, but the more I try, the less my body is inclined to rest. I roll over, grab the clock off my nightstand and check it. The numbers on the face of it shine so brightly in this dark bedroom. The blinding red numbers pierce through the darkness and peer at me. I've been checking it every fifteen minutes since midnight. It's like I've been in a horizontal dance all night. Rolling, tossing, reaching, checking, squinting and repeating- I dance. Additionally, if my life were a musical, it would be set to the tango with all the twisting and turning under the covers.

When, I check the time again, I notice it's already 5 o'clock in the morning. Going to sleep doesn't make sense, at this point, since my alarm is set to go off in forty-five minutes. It's better for me to get up and prepare for the long tedious day of showing homes. First, I have to get a mile run in before my neighbors are out and about couple-jogging on my usual route. It's difficult watching the lovey-dovey couples exercising and chatting away looking happy while I'm alone. So, I try to get my run in before any smiling faces notice me and I have to waste time pretending to be neighborly.

Afterward I'll head back home to the shower, grab a quick bite before I'm off to the office to print out a suitable list of properties to show to the client. "Sounds like a plan," I say while smiling at the darkness. This client has been searching for a property for her soon to be blended family, for the past six months. I have to hunker down and help her find a house. A commission could sure come in handy right now; besides, it helps me get back on track and focus on something other than Brian.

Moreover, five years ago I was featured in the *Realtor Magazine* after receiving the distinguished 30 Under 30 Awards for exceptional young realtors. This year I am being nominated for the NATIONAL ASSOCIATION OF REALTORS' New Jersey REALTOR of the Year Award which, if chosen, will be presented to me during the annual REALTORS Conference & Expo in November. All I have to do is focus on my career and eliminate all distractions.

"Ok, Arianna back to the task at hand." I say as I sit up in the bed and grab my cell phone to text Brian. "Does texting count as reaching out?" I say it out loud. "Not by Dr. Staten's standards." I quickly answered. "Girl you know you're losing it, when you start sitting in the dark talking to yourself. Get... it... together and just text *the* man! Then you can focus on your career." I whisper.

Hey Bri, It's Arianna. Long time, no hear. If you get a minute, would love to chat- just to catch up. Lemme know. Thx. :-0 A

I press send with a little hesitation as I roll out of bed and head to the bathroom to shower. Within seconds I hear my cell phone chime. *Can that be Brian already? Impossible. It's too early—why isn't he still asleep?*

I lean against my bathroom door- inhaling the woodsy fragrance of the pine. The smell calms my nerves, which I love. I know, as I pressed send there's a slim chance of Brian responding but imagine nothing beyond that. What should I do now? What did he say? Should I even check the message? There's a shooting pain in my stomach making its way through my insides to my chest and throat. Closing my eyes with my forehead and nose resting gently against the wood door, I inhale the pine one more time deeply, then exhale. *Relax Arianna.*

Reaching for the knob, I pull it open, run, and jump on the bed and grab the phone. It vibrates and chimes again. "Oh no!" I say to the darkness. I drop the phone without looking at it. "Just pick it up silly and read it."

Hey. Whatcha doin up so early? Waiting for the train? Lol. I'm free at noon. Lunch? Call u ltr.

I switch the phone to vibrate; then, drop it back on the bed. "Now what?" I say massaging my temples with my right fore-finger and thumb. "Shake it off! You are going to be Realtor of the Year gurl- make it happen." I live in the darkness a little longer before heading to the bright lights awaiting me in the bathroom.

∞∞∞

I head to the restaurant about thirty minutes early. We decide on the Cheesecake Factory as a symbolic gesture. It is the place where we had our first date. I love anything sweet as long as it has chocolate in it and Brian just loves good food. When I give the hostess my last name, she gives me a black plastic dial that will flash a bright red light and buzz three times when our table is ready.

The Cheesecake Factory is always busy, arriving early gives me enough time to find an empty seat or bench to sit on while Brian and I wait; otherwise, one of us will have to stand or awkwardly try to balance against the constantly swinging front door of the restaurant. Also, it gives me time to mentally prepare myself before I see him.

The restaurant is semi busy, which takes the edge off. Crowded enough to make me feel comfortable in case Brian is furious with me. He tries to maintain a drama-free life as possible. He'd never scream at me in such a public place and bring extra attention to us. And yet it's not overcrowded either. It's a good space. Intimate even-if we are seated in one of those corner booths with the decorative mini lamp in the center of the table.

He'd feel like he's being drowned out by the noise, if I chose a location where I couldn't hear a word he says. I wonder if Brian still loves me. Or if he really misses me and is, therefore, genuinely happy to see me. *Will he show up?* But the question that plagues my mind the most is: *Why did I ever agree to have lunch with him in that blasted text message?*

111

I twiddle my thumbs and tap my fingers repetitively on the dark wood bench that I'm occupying while I wait for my dial to flash and buzz. "What are you going to say? What are you going to say?" I say when I see Brian push his way through the restaurant door.

When Brian notices me the corners of his mouth raise to let out a huge smile. My heart throbs. He's deliciously dressed in some slim fit navy dress pants, and a pinstripe shirt and a fancy tie which I assume are all Hugo Boss- since he told me that's his favorite designer. I squeeze the dial I'm holding and raise it in the air to gesture for him to head in my direction. At the moment, I wish I had chosen a different more secluded rendezvous spot, for our first encounter in months because I want to grab his yumminess and devour him with my tongue of love.

There is seriousness in his eyes. Although he is looking directly at me I can see the wheels churning in his mind. Brian quickly steps toward me and his long legs shorten the distance between us in seconds. His breathing is steady as he reaches out to hug me. I sink into his arms; then, try to balance on my heels and push myself from his embrace.

"Hey there." I say taking two steps back.

"Hey there back at you." Brian smiles at me. "It's been a minute since we've spoken- eh."

"I know. I have been meaning to call you." The red dial vibrates in my hands. "Perfect timing." I raise the dial to show Brian the blinking lights. "We're up."

"Cool. Lead the way." He says.

I rub my lips together and instinctively lick them.

"Hungry much?"

When the corners of his mouth and left eyebrow raise, I start to relax. *He still loves me.* "No. Be quiet. You're always such a jokester."

I raise the vibrating dial in the view of a woman standing behind the hostess station across the lobby. When our eyes catch, she gives me a nod. She whispers in the ear of the hostess standing next to her who looks in my direction and smiles too. A hostess wearing a crisp white button-down shirt and black mini skirt grabs two Cheesecake Factory menus and beckons for us to follow her.

"Welcome to the Cheesecake Factory. My name is Chrisley. Follow me. I will take you to your seat."

Brian and I followed her in silence. She dips through the tables of chit-chatting foodies easily while I stumble my way clumsily. I look down at the chattering smiling faces apologetically each time I hip-bump them while trying to criss cross through the restaurant in pursuit of the hostess, Chrisley. Brian strolls behind me unaffected by the noise, people, or my clumsiness. When she looks back at us to make sure we are keeping up, I give her a half-baked smile as I brush up against another seated person.

She leads us to a semi secluded corner booth toward the back left side of the restaurant near the bar. An ideal spot.

"Your waitress will be with you shortly." Chrisley says with a smile. Then, without waiting for our response, she quickly turns and jets back toward her ever increasingly busy hostess station. I see the back of her bobbing ponytail as she maneuvers through a sea of people waving blinking red dials and grinning at her.

I slid in on the left side of the booth close enough to the wall to lean against it and set my purse down next to my left thigh. Brian plants himself across from me, sliding in close to the wall so he is positioned directly in front of me. After he sits he reaches across the table to take my hand.

"So how have you been?" He asks.

"I've been good and you?"

"It's been a minute since I've heard from you. What have you been up to?"

"Let's not talk about me just yet. How's the great negotiator?"

Brian looks at me and squints his eyes. "Nah, you first. How have you been?"

"Busy working," I say because I think it's the easiest response to build this undoubtedly awkward conversation off of.

A waitress stands over us smiling with her order pad and pen waiting silently to take our beverage and lunch orders. "Hi my name is Mariah. I will be your server today. Do you need a few minutes to look over the menu before I take your order?" She asks.

Brian and I know the Cheesecake Factory menu all too well so there's no need for us to study it.

Saying that, his mouth widens to show his pearly white teeth, and his dimples poke through the middle of his cheeks like craters. "I'll have the Miso Salmon with snow peas and white rice and..." He pauses. "The lovely lady will have the Seared Tuna Tataki Salad with extra vinaigrette on the side. Oh and one raspberry lemonade. Water for me." Then, he covers the side of his mouth with his hand and leans toward the waitress in a fake whisper, "She likes to keep it lite so she'll have room for a slice of Chocolate Mousse Cheesecake."

I quickly slap his menu as he hands it to the waitress and one of its plastic corners smacks him right in the center of his dimple. The menu fumbles into the waitress' hand who catches it before it can fall onto the table.

"Be nice you." I say jumbling my words as usual.

"What?" He says; then, winks at the waitress who walks away smiling.

"You have not changed, sir."

"Yes I have. Just a little."

"To what should I attribute the change?"

"Life. I think I've grown since you've seen me last."

Our waitress brings our drinks and sets them on the table in front of us. I sip on my raspberry lemonade while Brian swirls the ice chips around in his glass before gulping his water. While, I sit in the booth as still as possible trying to stall time. I have follow-up questions about how he has grown and what he meant by "life" changing him. But, I just need a few more minutes to breathe and collect my thoughts before we go down the road of the more serious conversation topics I know he's craving to discuss. "So what do you mean by you've grown since-"

"Uh huh beautiful... back to the subject at hand. Busy working eh?" He asks abruptly.

"Yes extremely. I'm up for an award that I really want. It's nonstop to make it happen."

"What kind of award?"

"I'd tell you but I don't want to jinx it- you know."

"So this mystery award has been taking up all of your time- huh?"

"Yes. Most of it."

"Oh I see. It's keeping you too busy to even pick up the phone to call or answer one text—huh?" Brian looks at me like he's searching my depth for the truth. This time he doesn't smile, smirk or laugh.

"I have meant to.... Bri but-"

"But what, Arianna?" He asks in a low voice. "It has been months since we've spoken. Not one word from you."

"I know. I just didn't know how to tell you what's been going on with me." I'm relieved when another person from the wait staff hurries toward us balancing our food on his large black tray. "Ah! Our food is here." I speak louder than intended. Brian smirks at me, grabs his drop cloth and lays it on his lap. I grab my napkin and place it across my legs making sure to concentrate my eyes on the motion of my hands, instead of returning his gaze.

"Who had the Miso Salmon?" The waiter calls. Brian raises his finger. "Careful, it's hot." He says. "So that means the salad belongs to you."

I look up at the waiter and blink my eyes. "Yes. Thank you." I say; then, look over at Brian who is waiting impatiently for the waiter to finish and leave. "Can you ask our waitress to send over some bread and butter, please?" I say hoping the waiter doesn't rush off. But he does.

"Will do." He calls as he takes flight down the row of tables toward the back kitchen door.

I pull my salad to me and douse it with a heap of vinaigrette. I swish the tuna, greens, and wasabi around in my bowl.

"Really Arianna?"

"What?"

"I realize we were interrupted but can you finish with your explanation to me before you dive into your salad?" He takes his fork and knife in his hand and slices into his fish and slides a scoop of rice onto his fork. "See, I can eat and talk." He takes a forkful of the salmon and rice mixture.

"Like I said. I didn't know how to tell you."

"Tell me what? That you didn't want to be with me anymore or that I never really knew you? Or was it to tell me how much you were suffering in silence?"

When he starts reciting the words from my last text messages, I know he's livid. But he doesn't raise his voice or change his tempo or tone. "I'm sorry. I know our last conversation could have made you a little confused." I say.

"A little Arianna?" He releases the grip on my hand. "You sent me a text that you "suffered in silence" and the last time we spent the night together we went to bed with everything being fine, soon after, I woke up to you sitting on the edge of the bed in your nightgown dazed. For an hour I tried to talk to you while you sat there. When you finally decide to say something to me- it's: you don't know me, and you never did. What the HELL, Arianna."

He barks out the word hell and I lower my eyes so I can't see the pain he is feeling. "I can understand your trepidation. But then why invite me to lunch. Why would you even want to see me? I can see how upset you are, Brian."

"Because, I want to know what happened. How did we go from being good to bad so quickly?"

"I... I-" I have a response but the words are lost in my thoughts. I can't manage to get them out.

"You know Arianna, I learn more about you through strangers than I hear from you."

"What do you mean?"

"What do I mean?"

"Yes"

"What do I mean? Arianna, you were in the hospital and you didn't even tell me!" He blurts outs.

I look up at him with bulging eyes, "Who told you?"

"Does that matter?"

"Yes, it matters to me." I try to recall the last few months and who I've spoken too. *Who knows? And who would have told him?*

"Hey," Brian snaps his fingers at me, "the- *who* doesn't matter. The point is that I found out from someone other than you."

"What was I supposed to say, Bri?"

"How about... Brian, I'm in the hospital. I nearly bled to death. Come by and be with me. I need you."

"I'd never say I needed you."

"Exactly you don't say anything. Strangers on the street confide in me more. You can't even tell me the name of the award you've been nominated for. That's sad."

"I don't know how to let-"

"Let me in? Let me get close to you? Let me know the real you? Which one?"

"All the above. It's too much."

"Yeah it's too much for you to share any part of yourself with me."

"Yes I need more time."

"How much time are we talking about? It's been two years-already."

"I don't know."

"Then I can't do this anymore. I want things you don't. Ain't this about a bi... I mean- blasted. Most women dream of men who want to share everything with them. But not Miss Arianna Dickerson, right. She needs more time."

I can't look him in the eyes. They desire too much. I lower my head again.

"Look at me?" He lifts my chin to expose my face.

So, I shut my eyes.

"Wow- nothing- huh? You have nothing for me?" He says.

I don't respond.

"Then why did you contact me, Arianna?"

"I wanted to hear your voice." I say honestly as I open my eyes to look at him. "And to let you know I was in the hospital."

"Cool. We've been talking for the past thirty minutes, so you accomplished that. Now I know about your hospital stay. I guess we're all good here. Is there anything else?" Brian stands up.

"Wait, aren't you going to stay for dessert?"

"Nah, I don't want dessert. I've had enough."

"But-" I grab his arm as I search for something to say. Something profound from my months of therapeutic sessions with Dr. Staten. This is unbelievably difficult. I know what he's waiting to hear. *Why can't you just say the words?*

"What is it Arianna? What do you want from me?"

"Nothing Brian. Forget about it." I pause. "I mean how are you doing?"

"Really?"

"I mean it's been a couple of months. Are you seeing anybody?"

"Seriously," Brian sits back down, "I've been talking to a young lady for a couple of weeks, actually. Nothing serious though. Just someone I know from work who's been trying to get with me for a while." He touches my hand. "I thought I already had a woman in my life. Obviously things change. I was hoping that this lunch reconnect would let me know where you and I stood. I was hoping to come here and see you and have you answer the lingering questions I had the past couple of months. Hoping we'd fix us or whatever was broken." He lets out a heavy breath, "Guess not."

"Well Bri- if you're happy then I'm happy for you."

"Seriously, that's all I get? You didn't hear a word I just said?"

"What do you want me to say? You're with someone else now."

"Nothing, Arianna. Do what you do--say nothing." Brian wiggles his hand from my grip. "I have to go. Yeah, I guess I'm happy enough. Anyway, I have a meeting in thirty that I still need to prepare for."

"Oh...ok. I understand, Bri." I say. "Perhaps, I can call you later?"

"Why Arianna?" He takes his keys from his pocket and pulls out his wallet. "You gonna stay? At least have a slice of the Chocolate Mousse Cheesecake while you're here." He places a fifty-dollar bill on the table. "That should cover everything."

"You don't have to." I say.

He grins at me, leans in and kisses my forehead. "Bye Miss Dickerson. Good luck on the award."

I smile up at Brian and watch his smooth quick step through the front lobby. He doesn't look back at me once. I watch him as long as I can until the glimpse of him fades.

I sit in the half empty booth scanning the restaurant and wondering if the other conversations between the couples, co-workers or family members will end as horribly as mine did. But from the intimate embraces, smiles and laughter, I think they will end blissfully. My love life is the only car wreck on the planet.

"Will there be anything else?" Mariah the waitress with the crisp white shirt and black pants who is standing over me asks.

"A slice of your Chocolate Mousse Cheesecake please."

"Will you need two spoons?" She asks, pointing to the empty space where Brian sat. "For your friend? Or should I come back for his order?"

I look across the table and imagine him still sitting there. "Two spoons will be fine, thanks." I said to the waitress. "He'll be back."

As, she walks away I pick up my cell phone to call the only person I believe will help:

"Hi Dr. Staten. I'm so glad I got your voicemail. I'd hate to hear the disappointment in your voice. I tried reaching out to Brian, as requested. It didn't go well at all. As a matter of fact, it was horrible. He's moved on. So I let him go. What do I do now?"

12

GROUP SESSION

∞**DR. STATEN ARRANGED** the chairs to form a makeshift group circle. Timothy lands in the chair to her right and Arianna slips in the chair about a foot away from Dr. Staten's left side, closest to a set of large windows.

"It's been a while. How are things? How difficult were the assignments regarding your loved ones? I know there were a few hiccups all around. Any thoughts?"

Timothy leans back in the chair, body slouched, with his head down- staring at the speckled rug underneath his feet. Arianna is silent and stiff like a statue made of cement blocks.

"So I see. Nothing to say? This is the most subdued I've seen either of you."

The room is silent aside from the brief noise Arianna's chair makes when she scoots it an inch to the left to look out the window at the large red oak trees lining the narrow outer pathway to the office.

"You know, if I drop a pin on the floor it will come crashing down in a loud echoing boom as it lands, from all the empty space in the room." Dr. Staten says.

"I already told you, doc." Timothy says breaking the silence. "The incident with my parents was atrocious. There's no recovering in the aftermath. Melissa and I argued and..."

"Then what?"

"You know what. I am my father's child and all the horrors that come with it.... so she left."

"That's how you rationalize things in your head? Or justify the things you do?"

"Yes."

"That is discouraging. Sad even."

"What does that mean?" Timothy asks, looking perplexed, hid brows knit together and fingers fiddling.

"There are some absolutes in life you have to understand. One is that you never put your hands on anyone in anger. Period. You leave. Walk away. If walking doesn't work then run."

"You said some absolutes- any others?" Timothy asks with an air of sarcasm.

Dr. Staten challenges him, "What did you call your father before when he hit your mother?"

He clasps his hands in front of him, interlocking his fingers and resting his chin on his thumbs. "I said he was nothing but a loudmouth bully and a coward."

"Right? How are your actions toward Melissa any different?"

"I'm working on that. I'm here aren't I?" He snarls.

"Yes. Now we have to discuss some real solutions so you don't lash out at the women in your life every time you get infuriated."

"What do you suggest? You're a professional, right?"

"You tell me. What's one solution for you, when the anger builds?"

"Walk away?"

"Is that a question or a solution?"

Timothy shrugs his shoulders. "It's a response easier said than done."

"Have you ever tried?"

He glares at her.

"No need to scowl. I'm just asking a question. Timothy, what will you do differently the next time the anger builds- besides lashing out like a bully or a coward? Your words not mine."

"Walk away." He says.

"That's it. Remember the most powerful role model in any family is the same sex parent."

"Well. I guess I'm working at a huge disadvantage then."

"Me too," Arianna agrees. "I'm all screwed up- because my parents are gone." She stares out the window still looking past both Timothy and Dr. Staten toward the large red oak tree. "I mean dead."

124

Timothy looks at her but Arianna ignores him. "I bet your father would have been a better role model than the one I have." He says.

"Perhaps." She says haphazardly.

Dr. Staten leans in toward Timothy, "Another absolute is you have a choice. You can choose to go a different direction than your father, Timothy."

"How?"

"Continue coming to our meetings. So we can continue to examine your past and present challenges until you're in the healthy place you long for. Until the decision to walk away or remain calm is the only clear choice." Dr. Staten snaps her fingers at Arianna. "Our sessions allow you both to face your challenges and ultimately learn to forgive." She pauses. "Gandhi said the weak can never forgive. Forgiveness is an attribute of the strong. Which are you?"

"I'm no Gandhi." Timothy says.

"Neither am I." Arianna chimes in; finally, returning her focus to the group, instead of the swaying branches of the red oak scratching against the window. "But I want to be strong. Living like this is leading us nowhere, Timothy. Except down a path of loneliness. You are not an island. And I want to be strong enough to move on already."

"I know. That's why I'm here instead of out there. I dread sitting in the hot seat session after session-- trying." Timothy says.

"You're absolutely correct," Dr. Staten says. "You come here week after week, session after session trying to learn how to handle life better. As I said on day one this is a process. All you have to do is remain in the process and apply the solutions. It will get better."

"Walk away. Forgive. Those are loaded words." Timothy says.

"Have you ever tried it before?"

"No."

"Well then yes- they are loaded indeed and powerful words when they become actions. Start simple. Just walk away the next time you feel the anger building. See how it goes. I'll venture to say that once you remove yourself from the tumultuous situation and find your solace in a place of solitude, you'll see the choices clearer." Dr. Staten steadies her focus on Timothy.

"What about me, Dr. Staten? My challenge is not being so angry that I strike other people." Arianna looks at Timothy. "Sorry, I didn't mean-"

"Not a problem. I understand, you didn't mean to offend." Timothy reassures her.

"Yes, exactly."

Dr. Staten interrupts. "No, it's not. But who feels the physical thrust of your blow, when you're overwhelmed?"

"Me or myself? I don't know which is grammatically correct to say."

"It would be... *I do.*" Timothy sits up in his chair sticks out his chest proudly when Arianna looks at him. "You'd know all about proper syntax if your mother were the acclaimed English teacher- Priscilla Fox of the Childress Preparatory School. Grammar is the one thing she drilled into our heads while my father knocked her aside hers"

"Sorry." Arianna says in a low voice. "I wasn't trying to dredge up-"

"No problem," He responds before Arianna completes her apology.

"Not to interrupt the English lesson," Dr. Staten breaks through the awkwardness, "but you're in the habit of lashing out in two ways. First, you hurt yourself physically, and second, you hurt the ones you love with words. Therefore, this applies to you as well. Before you react, choose to take a moment. Take a walk. Remove yourself from the situation and find a different way to escape." She pauses. "Neither of you have to be Gandhi. You do, however, have to learn to forgive so you'll become a stronger version of yourself."

"I'll try anything at this point." Arianna says.

"Me too." Timothy nods at Dr. Staten, then smiles. "But how about I take it one step further and never speak to my parents or Melissa again that way there will be no source of frustration for me to lash out."

"That's merely glossing over the problem while it lies dormant. Eventually it resurfaces." Dr. Staten doesn't return his smile. "How about we work toward-"

"I know... I know- solutions, right." He says.

"Yes, solutions." Dr. Staten purses her lips and looks up. "I know you both had less than perfect outcomes in the last assignment I gave you. How about a "redo"- or do-over? Timothy, your Princeton exhibit seems like the perfect venue to reconnect with your mother. And Arianna how about inviting Brian out again. This time somewhere new so you can establish new memories."

"I don't know if I'm ready to see my mother, yet." Timothy says.

"Then write. If a face to face is not possible. You can always put it in a letter. Which to some seems less invasive." Dr. Staten says.

"Where do I take him? Cause, I don't have the faintest idea." Arianna asks.

"Oh, you should try Bahama Breeze at the Cherry Hill Mall. It's a really lively spot with great food." Timothy suggests.

"Well then it sounds like you both have a plan. Let's make this happen before our next session." Dr. Staten says.

"I can't do any worse." Arianna stood up from her chair and said. "Till next we meet."

"Sounds very poetic Arianna." Dr. Staten says.

"Later doc." Timothy called looking back at her with sadness.

"Your valediction is predictable Timothy. Needs work." Dr. Staten tried to encourage him to smile. When his eyes were still gloomy, she wondered if he could cope with what was about to happen.

13

SOMETIMES THE ANSWER IS NO

∞WEEKS AFTER THE luncheon fiasco, I call Brian asking for a "redo"- as Dr. Staten suggests. I don't want another lunch date at a familiar spot, so I set up a dinner date at this nice Caribbean restaurant in Cherry Hill I recently heard about. It's supposed to have great food, live music and an upbeat atmosphere. A change in scenery for both Brian and I might be what we need right now. When I speak with Dr. Staten, she asks me what I would do to see if Brian and I still have a chance. I shock myself when the words: whatever it takes... I only want to be with him- spews out my mouth and into the ether for everyone to hear. That's when Dr. Staten suggests I try again. This time allowing myself to expose all to him. Shock number two comes when I agree to do it, as well. I don't know the first thing about pouring out my soul or any other part of me, but a more courageous me surface the moment Brian walks out, leaving a trail of the pieces of my heart, from the booth to the front door at our restaurant the Cheesecake Factory. I finish my cheesecake with a new determination fueled by a desire to get my heart back along with Brian's love.

Now, all I think about is fighting for him. Win. Lose. Or Draw. I'm not going down without first collecting my brokenness and spreading it across the table- we'll see if Brian can master the jigsaw puzzle that is my life and figure out how to put me back together. I know, it's a lot- undoable even. If he's successful, perhaps there's hope for us- and this love thing.

I called him to schedule the dinner date. I don't let my nerves take over me. At first, he's standoffish but then I hear, "of course beautiful" as only he can say in a way that makes my toes curl as fluttering butterflies intrude my insides. Hence, I set our meet-up time for 8:00 PM, that gives us both enough time to travel down the I95 to the I295 to Rt.73 straight to Cherry Hill. *This Bahama Breeze restaurant better live up to all the hype- or I'm going to destroy Timothy. I can't believe I'm taking advice from a person who is as damaged as me.*

∞∞∞∞

It's torrential rain as I head to Bahama Breeze to meet Brian. I plug my USB into the car media player and turn on my Bluetooth, so I can hear exactly who I want to hear, when I want to hear them, as many times as I want to hear them- while I drive. I created a long list of love songs on my iTunes playlist of R&B, contemporary gospel and smooth tunes continuously musing about true love. The songs will help soothe my soul and prepare my heart for the Brian-Arianna matchup at the restaurant. It also gives me the audacity to hope for our fiery dialogue and impassioned glances between two lovers. Although I am nervous, I am more anxiety-stricken than anything.

The rain beats aggressively against my windshield. I turn the wipers to the quickest position, so I can see through the rain assault and focus on the road. I'm glad the I95 is mostly clear so the flow of traffic is steady. I'm not accustomed to driving in the rain but I'm on a mission. So, I push on through the winds and rain bobbing my head to the rhythmic beat of the music and mouth as many of the words to the songs I can remember. Surprisingly, I am calmer than imagined, when thoughts of reconciliation with Brian make me smile.

When the remix of Al Green's "Let's Stay Together" starts to play, at the exact moment I'm smiling about Brian's and our promising future, I take the perfect timing as a sign from God that he and I are going to make it. *But what if he changes his mind and doesn't show? What if he decides he wants to stay with the woman from work? What if he doesn't love me back?* I stop smiling at the thought of it.

132

Now, it's raining inside the car, too. This time, the torrential waves came from my eyes. Even so, I use my right hand as a windshield wiper to clear away the tears. I pulled up to the restaurant, turn the car off- so, the love songs stop playing- and sit in the driver's seat alone and deflated. When I glance down at my wristwatch and notice it's a quarter to eight, I have a few minutes to decide my next move. "You're here now Arianna, just go inside." I encourage myself. "He'll be here."

It's 8 o'clock when I, finally, decide to go inside the restaurant. Since I made reservations and it's not too busy, there is no wait time so, no need for plastic chiming dials like at the Cheesecake Factory. *Another positive sign.* The hostess directs me to a table near the Caribbean band who's preparing on stage. Quickly, I scan the room to see if there are many couples around and notice tons, so I smile. I smell coriander, sage, cayenne, and other familiar spices used in Caribbean dishes- good food. At the table next to me, the couple ordered a great smelling red snapper dish, they were scoffing down, which makes me think Timothy's choice in the restaurant might be spot on. I am happy again and start to relax. Then, I look down at my wrist watch and see it's 8:20 pm "It's raining Arianna. Give it ten more minutes." I say it out loud. "He'll be here."

After twenty minutes more, two appetizers and a drink called the Painkiller, which I ordered Virgin style- I recognize that I've been stood up. I charge my bill and walk out into the downpour toward my car and head home. No need to connect my USB or hook up my iTunes playlist, there's no love here. "I told you." I mumble; then, drive the long way back in silence.

When I make it home, I pull off my wet clothes and shoes and head to my den. I can't accept that it's over between Brian and I, without first having a chance to explain a few things to him. I grab a felt pen, a piece of canary linen paper and write. What I think will be simple talking points turn into letters... an ode to Brian.

Dear Bri,

I think I suffer from giving too much information. If I could go back in time to retract my statements last month, we'd still be together. Imagine I didn't say what I said or do what I did. Simply, let things be; instead, and progress naturally without trying to be the fixer. But I was born a fixer. From a teenager to now, everything I do is to try to fix what is wrong. I always make things worse.

If I could go back in time like they do in the movies, I'd hop in a time machine and make different choices. Then, I wouldn't be sitting alone in my den surrounded by dull lighting, brushing tears off my cheeks at the thought of your not showing up tonight. Why didn't you show? I'd call for a "do-over" of our luncheon date. A "do-over" of the conversation in my bedroom. There wouldn't be a bucket list of mistakes piling up in my heart-from the last two days, now the last two years. No, what, I mean are the last two decades of my life. Back in time, I would save us.

I realize this is coming out all topsy-turvy, distorted and unintentionally jumbled, but you know me. What I'm trying to say is sorry. I'm asking for a live time "do over" because time machines don't exist. Chances are I'm too late. Am I? Or is there still time to make us right? I love you. There, I said it!

Love, A

∞∞∞∞∞

Still, I hold on to his letter which is stuffed in the pocket of my desk drawer in the den. I take it out to read aloud a few times before slipping it in a white envelope addressed and stamped to send to Brian.

When I wrote it the other day, I assumed I'd take it to the post office to send it next day air, paying the extra fee to ensure he'll have to sign for it upon delivery- I simply lack the courage to follow through with anything.

I miss my group session with Dr. Staten and Timothy. It's not as if the sessions are helping- if they were Brian and I would be together.

I blame her. She's the one that made me tell the story and made me believe I was mending- or even capable of getting better. She told me to "let him in" and to "let him see you distressed full of jabs like the old hickory chair" and the biggest whopper- the colossal falsification of all- the one I hear ringing in my ears daily "it's not your fault." Well, she was wrong. It's obvious I am at fault. Why else did Brian stand me up? I listened to her and I ended up sitting in a restaurant cold, wet and alone. So, I stay home from our group, it's her turn to see what it feels like to be stood up.

I'm stuck. I need to send the letter. Should I send the letter? She'd encourage me to send it. I'll send it tomorrow.

∞∞∞∞

The phone rings three times before I pick up.

"Hello, may I speak with Ms. Arianna Dickerson?"

"Yes, that's me."

"Are you sitting down?"

I pause to look at the phone. I don't like those words. It's going to be bad news.

"I'm the ER nurse at Mountainside General Hospital. My name is Nurse Agnes. Your name and number were found in the pants' pocket of a Mr. Brian Maxwell," the even toned voice on the other end of the phone explains.

That's the only part of the conversation that comes through clear. Cause, I go numb. My mind is blank. Everything comes through my ear gate like junk mail- waiting in the queue. Just a series of jumbled words mixed and spilling through the voice of a stranger with a familiar name. An ER nurse who says she remembers me from a previous hospital stay. I can't remember her.

She said something about a crash on a horribly rainy night causing severe head trauma, and she kept repeating Brian's name to trigger or elicit a response. I am too numb. I feel nothing. Then, there is something about the hospital and Brian's surgery. It's critical. The last thing I hear is the word coma. I shut my eyes as tight as possible and drop the phone when I use my hands to cover my ears. I try inhaling through my nose and exhaling through my mouth regularly to steady my breathing.

As I pick up the phone and put it back to my ears, I hear the ER nurse still clamoring away about Brian's grave state. *What is her name? Stop calling her the ER nurse? She told you her name- try to remember?* I need the chaos of the ER nurses' jumbled words to become sentences I comprehend. But every time I think I grasp the parts of the conversation- my thoughts crash against my mind like an ocean crashing against the shore. Mere, waves of nothingness. *I got it.*

"Nurse Agnes... people I love shouldn't drive," is all, I can fathom to blurt out.

"Excuse me." Nurse Agnes asks.

I go numb and quiet again.

I slam the cell phone onto the table when I hang up and reach for the edge of the kitchen table to lean against, so I can sit securely on one of the chairs.

My weak hand slips its grip, slides off the table, and I teeter totter to the ground. *I'm falling...no, I'm dying.* I grab my chest with one hand and start pounding the palm of my other hand against my head. Pounding away till, the ringing sound in my head is louder than the dreaded words of Nurse Agnes. My head hurts. My heart stings with piercing pain and feeling of weightlessness that comes over me as my body slips further against the floor. I let my hands drop. I curl up into a ball on the cold kitchen floor and wail, "Brian, oh God, No!"

14

WRITE THE LETTER, RIGHT!

∞JUST WRITE THE letter. Just write the letter. Don't worry about the perfect salutation or if it's grammatically correct- just put pen to paper and see what comes of it.

Timothy tries to encourage himself, so he can check one more item off the TO DO LIST for his life, which he believes Dr. Staten created. If he doesn't follow directions as seemingly simple as seeing "that woman" or her husband again- he won't get to a healthier place. For the sake of his mental and emotional health, he must get a grip, pull himself together and do the assignment.

He'll have to bite the bullet... grab the bull by the horns..., or a series of other choice idioms he tells himself as motivation to "go for it" no matter what. Even if it seems ridiculous, "reductio ad absurdum" the Latin phrase, he instantaneously recollects his mother using to describe something absurd, with an immense desire to love or be loved, he'll do this.

He balls up the first couple of sheets of paper and tosses them on the ground. A ritual he uses when starting on a new canvass or laying out the landscape. The first sketches are always tossed. So, he will approach the invitation the same way. He leans against the wooden back of the high studio stool and swishes from left to right as a distraction but quickly jerks himself forward clutching the paper. Just write it to her. Not to him. This gesture will be the only invitation, then, the balls in her court. "Another idiom. Gee Tim, you are as predictable as Dr. Staten believes." He says, then, grits his teeth.

Dear Priscilla/ Mother,

I send this letter to you under duress (the therapist feels my reaching out to you is crucial at this juncture in my therapy). As you know, my exhibition is in a few weeks and I would appreciate it if you attended. I realize our last encounter did not fare well – for either of us- and this event will be a chance for you and I too start anew.

You'll get to see what occupies my time. Isn't that a good gesture on my part? Afterwards we can grab a bite to eat and talk, perhaps. The formal invitation ticket including dates, time, and directions is enclosed.

I truly hope you can make it. I think this event could be a positive step for us.

Sincerely,
Timothy Y. Fox

p.s. - I almost forgot, there's only one invite included, which means you'll have to attend solo.

He finishes the letter and places it on top of a pile of papers on the edge of his table. He's been working on, what should have been, this simple letter of invitation for over an hour.

"No more thinking of that woman." He gives one loud clap, and rubs his hands together. He pulls his pencils, oils, charcoal, and pastels from the paint drawer on the center shelf of his studio table, whirls around in his chair, then stretches a clean piece of canvas across the tabletop.

He flips his drawing paper onto a clean sheet in case he feels more like sketching than painting. The sheet leans sturdily against the easel next to him. "Now let's see. All you need is one final piece. Something strong enough to complete the collection." He claps his hands again. "C'mon you can do this."

Unconsciously, he reaches for the cinnamon, dark brown, red, yellow, green, white paints and black charcoal- mixing and blending them until they are a different shade. He stares through the blank page until an invisible image appears. It's of his mother's face, hair, and dress.

It's all he can see. That's it. His final piece is a tribute to his mother. Why her? He's not sure why- but her image haunts him now. She stands there, pregnant yet empty. Alive yet, soul-less. Trying. Yearning. Juggling life as best she can. A picture of that woman- is all he can paint.

His hands glide across the page in a hypnotic rhythm. Quick strokes against the canvas, dipping into the mixed paint until it's a perfect blend as it passes from his brush to the canvas. He's lost in the work and strokes like a man possessed. He sits in front of the once blank canvass working it with colors and charcoal for her hair until he's able to stop. It takes five hours before his mind, body and soul release him.

He runs quickly to the bathroom and splashes a handful of cold water on his face. "What the hell just happened? Why do you need to add her?" he whispers and breathes out hard.

When he gets back to his studio chair, he picks up the canvass to look it over. Unpredictably, it is one of the strongest pieces he's ever created. It complements his other pieces and is a powerful conclusion to his exhibit. Timothy lays the painting down and wipes his charcoal and paint filled hands on his pant leg. Additionally, he grabs the charcoal and brushes it against the canvas to define the hair on the image he's created. He also uses it to develop the emptiness and soullessness of the person he portrays by drawing circular pits in the center of the image.

He turns on the table lamp and twists its bendable metal neck down toward the canvass, so he can see while he adjusts his work. The extra light helps him see all the imperfections in the hair, the face, and even the dress that drapes along the body of the image as she juggles her life.

"Almost done," he says, rubbing his eyes "just a few more touches then I need to let it sit overnight and come back to it with a fresh set of eyes in the morning."

He drops his tools, grabs the letter from off the top of the pile of papers on his desk and opens it to add an extra line or two

P.P.S. - There is a special piece. The main piece in my collection that is inspired and dedicated to you. I would like to hear your thoughts on it. I'm excited to show it to you. Also, disregard what I wrote earlier about attending solo. You may bring a "plus one" if you'd like.

After he finishes, he folds the letter, turns off the table lamp and swirls around in his chair once more. "Tomorrow, I'll be done with her." He says as he walks out the studio fanning himself with his mother's invitation letter. "Now all I need to do is mail this."

15

ANY DAY NOW

∞**I SLIDE A** chair next to Brian's bed and plant myself in it as the pudgy waist nurse instructs. I'm not convinced it will help him, even so, I try to do as she says, "Talk to him Miss Arianna." Nurse Agnes still struggles with how to say my name informally. "Let him hear your voice and perhaps that will help him find his way back to consciousness." She says.

"But he's in a coma. Everything I've read says if he's in a coma, he's unconscious and unresponsive."

"I know that's what the books say and anyone with an internet connection can find that out on google."

"Yet you say talk to him anyway?"

"Yes. What if the books or the internet are incorrect and although he's unresponsive, he can still hear you?"

"Ok." I look at this seemingly empty shell of a man lying in the hospital bed. "I'll try. What should I say? Anything in particular?" I ask, wanting to get it right.

"Whatever you want. There's no set dialogue."

"And this will help him?"

"I truly believe so."

"Are you sure?"

"I'm sure there's no harm in trying, right?"

So that's what I do.

At first, I just used simple conversational words, nothing intimate-nothing too telling. He lies still all tubed up to machines, so he can breathe. Then, I reminded him of this hilarious joke he told me some time ago. The one that keeps us laughing for hours to this day at the mention of it. Certainly, if even a glimpse of him remains in this shell, he'll wake up and laugh at my jokes. I'm that funny.

I hold his chilly hand gently in a mine, caressing it, hoping my warmth rubs off on him and calls him back to life. The incessant clatter of the machines are extremely loud though he is quiet. I hold onto him. This time talking in a more serious tone since the joke turned out to be an epic failure. I talk about our life together. Hopefully, this response helps because I keep talking. Any minute, he will wake up and acknowledge me.

That was three hours ago. Still, nothing.

∞∞∞∞

Three days pass and Brian hasn't come too. I'm beginning to doubt the need for my presence. Nothing changes. He lies in the bed comatose looking lifeless. It's insufferable. I try poking him in the side, when no one is looking, he doesn't move or jerk at all. I want to see the two craters in the sides of his cheeks he calls dimples- invade his face with a smile. Besides, it's getting more difficult for me to sit in this room, day after day, hour after hour waiting for him to open his eyes. There are too many memories which I try to drown out by increasing the volume of my voice while speaking to him.

I hate that there are plugs connecting to outlets, which connect machines to too many tubes, and the many tubes connect to Brian. He looks like an alien with tubes for tentacles. All so the doctor can monitor his heart, his brain activity, his breathing, feeding tubes poking in and out of him- Everything that keeps him alive. I don't have the strength to do this again. He has to survive. I don't know how anyone does this. But I can't leave. I remain bedside, constantly talking about everything fathomable, hoping to peak Brian's interest enough to awaken. Suddenly, a memory creeps its way through all the brain fog, and persistent clitter-clatter of the machines. *What if they ask you to decide like before?*

I look up and see Dr. Staten patrolling back and forth outside Brian's room, peeking in every so often to see if I'll ask her to come in. How did she even know I was here? Maybe Nurse Agnes? Dr. Staten is like a predator eyeing its prey and waiting to attack. She wants to pounce on me with words. She wants to sit next me- as if we were in the group and say, "Tell me Arianna, how does this make you feel?" I won't give her the satisfaction. Her predatory stroll won't distract me from Brian. He's my mission. No not now, while he's lying at deaths' door. I've disinvited her into my space. I call Sanctuary... Sanctuary... sanctuary- no psych docs allowed!

Today I am the therapist who calls the group to order. I will ask the tough, uncomfortable question, how does that make you feel? Every day, I'll question him repeatedly, until he responds. I don't need her help this time. She wants to spout quotes from Gandhi. Yeah right. Where is Gandhi now? There's only Brian and I here. That's what I'll tell her if she has the nerve to walk through this door. If she asks what I'm doing I'll say to coin a phrase from Gandhi, "I'm being the change, I wish to see in the world." Honestly, all I want to see at this moment is a conscious Brian Maxwell. Only that will change my world for the better.

I pull out my cell phone to text Aunt Maria for support:

Hi Auntie M, I'm in the hospital! What are you doing? A-

Seconds later my phone rings.
"Hello," I say.
"Ari-," The breathless voice calls out to me. "What happened? Are you ok? What hospital are you in?"
"Yes Auntie I'm fine." I pause to give her a chance to relax. "It's not me. I'm here visiting a friend. He's in the hospital."
"Oh my. What happened to your friend?"
"A car accident."
There is a short pause. "Ari-, I am sorry to hear that. I'm sure he'll be fine."
"What if he's not?"
"He will be, dear."
"I can't go," I wanted to remind her of my parent's tragic death.
"I know. I know." She says cutting me off. "If he wakes up, you'll be so thrilled. Think positive thoughts. He'll pull through."
"That's difficult to do."

147

"Where are you?"

"Mountainside Hospital." I hoped by giving short responses she would move on and end the conversation.

"Would you like me to come sit with you?"

I pause. For a moment it feels as if everything around me freezes.

"Arianna Maria Dickerson, my namesake," she called me by my full name when she's on the cusp of complete annoyances.

The sound of it jolts my body back into commission. "Auntie, I have to go. The doctor's coming?" I lied.

"Ok sweetie. Call me and let me know how your friend is doing. Arianna, when you came by the house a month ago why didn't you stay?"

"Auntie, I really have to go. Call you soon." I said and hung up before she could ask anything else. Last month was about Brian and I don't want her to judge him harshly. Especially knowing he's in this hospital bed now, battling for his life. I place the phone back in my pocket and lay my head on the edge of Brian's hospital bed. "Why is everything so difficult?" I mumble.

Perhaps, I'll bring the letter to the hospital tomorrow and read it to Brian. The one I keep tucked away in a stamped envelope in the desk drawer in my den. Perhaps when I read aloud to him, and he hears the sorrowful plea in my apologetic tone, he'll return to me.

16

IT'S TIME TO COME HOME

∞**SUNDAY MORNING** I get up early to head to church. Dr. Staten thinks being surrounded by people in a high spirited- church setting- experiencing something bigger than me, is exactly what I need these days. At first, I feel her suggestion is bizarre but after the long hospital stay by the seemingly lifeless Brian's bedside, a service, full of lively, highfalutin churchgoers may help.

I go from the sickening white walls of the hospital to vibrant red, green and gold flashing spot lights, lively music and hopeful characters worshiping in unison.

Pastor Jacobs' sermon is as intoxicating as his crisp white dress shirt with its gold embroidered sleeves, black jeans and shiny black and gold Addison Dress Shoes. He preaches about love and forgiveness similar to how Dr. Staten explains it to Timothy and I in the groups. Timothy secretly wished to be like Pastor Jacobs. He seemed to be a well- rounded man, intelligent and family oriented. His children adore him and he fortified them with gentle strength, unlike the family he grew up in.

"We cannot charge people for our Love." Pastor Jacobs says recollecting a story, "This woman told me she no longer loves her husband, in fact hates him and wants to see him hurt relentlessly, then leave him." He adds. "Then I said to her for two months show him love, treat him great, pour into him like never before- doing good. After two months leave him- without so much as a goodbye that will hurt him beyond repair. The woman, very excited about doing this hurtful thing to her husband, agreed to do as I proposed.

Furthermore, two months later, I went back to her and asked if she had done everything I told her and now left her husband? The woman said: No, I actually found out I still love him and never want to leave him. I say to her, you know what you did? You learned to put on love. The bible kind of love. And through loving him you learned to forgive as well."

Pastor Jacobs looks out to the congregation staring right in my direction. "As people searching for love, wanting to be loved, we are all still learning. Take it from me, success comes to those who learn to forgive." He says.

"Amen Pastor! You're preaching to me!" I call out; then quickly scan the room to see if anyone else notices my cry of conviction.

I see Timothy sitting in the catty corner from me, one row forward. I didn't even notice him when I sat down. He rubs on a folded piece of paper in his right hand. Every few minutes, he unfolds it, reads it, and stares at Pastor Jacobs. He must be contemplating a decision he hopes the sermon can inadvertently advise him on. Much like me.

There's no way for me to tell what he wrote down on that piece of paper from here. Still, I stretch as far up in my seat as possible, trying not to be too obvious, to get a glimpse of it. Is it the note for his mother, Dr. Staten spoke of during the last group session? I bet it is. I feel weird concentrating more on Timothy now than the sermon- he seems flummoxed. The next time I glance over at him, he catches me and smiles. He holds up the note with a strange sort of grin. Then, he folds the note and cradles it between his hands and points toward the cross at the front of the church.

"What?" I mouthed.

"Should I give this to her?"

"Who?"

"You know who." He raises an eyebrow and smirks at me.

I'm not sure how to respond. What if I say the wrong thing and make his relationship drama with his Mom worse? We're in a church for God sake and not in our weekly group session! He's asking me about his mother? How strange is that? I'm not a licensed therapist. Timothy is an odd fellow. He's sexy and smart, though odd is definitely the perfect word to describe him. "Why are you asking me?" I finally responded.

"I trust you." He mouths.

The words shock me. My eyes widen, and I show him nothing but teeth. "Wow. Thanks. I don't know?" I shrug my shoulders.

He points up toward the cross again and mouths, "Perhaps HE knows." He smiles.

"Perhaps." I smile back at him. A couple of times, I feel him looking back at me, and I try not to acknowledge him. I can't help but to glance in his direction unconsciously and each time we lock eyes.

"In the heart of every person is a cry for love. But, only the love of God truly satisfies." I hear Pastor Jacob's say. Although he's standing near me his words seem to echo.

Timothy is distracting me.

I shift in my seat, so I can face forward and focus only on Pastor Jacobs' sermon. "God loves you because of the cross. That's where HIS love is demonstrated. A love that can conquer anything. But you can't conquer what you can't confront!" He continues. "Remember these words, If I am the person who Jesus loves and HIS love conquers all then through HIS conquering love- I can love others correctly!"

Timothy seems mesmerized by Pastor Jacob. I think he's crying. Is he crying? I wish I could cry. Now, he's walking toward the altar among the masses. They throng to the foot of the altar most crying, others standing there gazing up at Pastor Jacobs like he's Jesus speaking to the multitude. I can only see the top of Timothy's head. He's just another speck in a sea of parishioners.

I wish Brian was here thinking that intently about me. Or, writing me notes, like Timothy writes to his always grammatically correct, probably thesaurus toting mother. Brian can't write or do anything at the moment. Life is too unfair. I close my eyes and drift away in my thoughts.

∞∞∞∞

After service, I see Dr. Staten sitting in the back of the church talking to a group of people. When she looks at me, I wave to her. I guess that was the invitation she was waiting for because as soon as I wave she leaves the group abruptly and rushes toward me.

"Oh no. I didn't mean to interrupt you." I say.

"I know. It's been a while since you attended the group so it was more important that I catch up with you than them." She says in her loquacious therapist way.

"Oh yeah, about that. I've been meaning to come back to group. As you know I've been in the hospital with Brian and when I'm not with him I've been working like a beast to sell a couple more properties."

"Right, you are a realtor. And yes I've seen you-"

"And," I cut her off, "I've been in contact with you via text, right? I even took your last suggestion to come to church today."

"All great steps. I think a group would be good for you, as well. Besides, I know someone who'd really like to see you again." She says pointing to Timothy who's sitting on the pew peering up at the cross.

"How's he doing?"

"Why don't you come to the group and ask him yourself." Some woman wearing a wide brim hat walks up to us and nudges Dr. Staten. "I know. I'm coming." She says to the intruder. "Arianna, will I see you on Friday?" She says in a low voice after pulling me in close to disguise her query in a hug. I figure she doesn't want the wide brim intruder to hear us.

"I'll try." Dr. Staten, grips me tighter. "I mean, yes. I'll be there."

She loosens her grip, "Great, now put it in your calendar. Hope you get another home sold. I have to go now. But text me if you need anything," she says as she walks away with the intruder tracking her steps.

"Will do. Thanks!" I called back.

I smile at the thought of Dr. Staten being stalked by the mysterious intruder who never introduces herself. Then, I look back to see if Timothy is still hanging around. He's not. He must've gotten his answer from above. For a moment my thoughts are happy which is short lived by the time I get to my car, and I realize I still have to visit Brian, today.

I rush home to print out a couple of new listings for potential clients and check on the weekend Open House. I ask a co-realtor, Evonne Atkinson, to cover for me. Evonne's, more like my assistant. She's cool. I like her work ethic and her quick development- under my tutelage. When I branch out and operate my brokerage firm, she'll be the person I take with me. She says there was an encouraging number of couples and families who walked through the property. There was even a repeat offender, a woman who showed up at the Saturday open house returned today and is walking through the house now. All very encouraging. I change my clothes, grab a bite to eat, then, it is back to Brian's bedside. On my way out the door, I grab Brian's letter to read to him.

"I hope this helps. I really hope this helps. This better help." I repeat it over and over again.

17

THERE IS HELP FOR THE WEARY

∞TIMOTHY SAT AT the end of the pew, looking back and spots Arianna on the next row back. He figures he should be paying close attention to the speaker, but she is very interesting. The fact that she's in church the same day and time as him, sitting in his vicinity, must be a sign from above directing him on what to do with this letter burning through the palm of his hand.

When he asks Arianna her thoughts, she seems confused and afraid to give him an answer. Nonetheless, he asks her because over the months, he has been accustomed to sharing with her in the group and likes the integrity of her responses. Today he feels she's overthinking and, therefore, of little help to him.

In between spying on his fellow therapy mate and contemplating whether to send his mother's letter, something Pastor Jacob's says hits him, "God loves you because of the cross. That's where HIS love is demonstrated. Love can conquer anything. But you can't conquer what you can't confront!"

So, true. I can't conquer what I won't confront. He thought as he squished the letter in his hand.

"Remember these words: If I am the person who Jesus loves and HIS love conquers all then through HIS conquering love I can love others correctly. I can conquer this!" says Pastor Jacobs.

Timothy sits upright. "If I can confront her, I know I can conquer this." He believes the pastor's words are earnest and true so he shifts focus away from the enticing Arianna and concentrates fully on the sermon.

He must pay attention and see what comes next.

159

"If you can change your mind, you can break anything that has a hold on you. The powerful force destroyed the road to healing. You're trying to move forward, and it keeps pulling you back. Please understand, your stronghold is in your head and until you climb up in your thought life and take control to destroy it, you'll never be Free!" The base in his voice bounces off the walls when he speaks into the microphone, vociferously causing the stencil pane glass windows to shudder. "If you're still angry...then you are still connected to your oppressor. What do you do when everything you relate to is connected to the oppressor? Sometimes your body comes out, but not the mind. Isn't it funny how after you leave something it looks better, all because the enemy has a way of giving you selective amnesia. Like the children of Israel, they forgot the oppression, all they remember is they were once in a place being fed and now, they are starving!"

"Amen, Pastor J," someone calls from the back of the sanctuary.

"We identify ourselves as the oppressed. Then, we don't know how to live outside of our oppression. It's simple, either you adapt to change, or you die. I say, give me liberty, you can keep death!" he said with such authority and conviction in his voice.

Then, wiping the sweat off his brow, he added, "you know you are finally free from a person, when you can see them and there is no response. The Pastor ends in a whisper, "you want to know what peace is? It's nothingness."

Timothy sits statuesquely while his insides burn from the incorrigible sting of Pastor Jacob's words. He's been waiting for a clear direction. Anything to give him some clue as to why he's going through what he's dealt with his entire life.

"It's time I step up to the plate. Be a better, healthier person" He says much louder than intended, an elderly woman on the pew next to him smiles and nods in agreement.

"I tell myself everyday Tim you are not going to be your father, you are going to be a better man than that!" He continues his confession to the elderly woman without even thinking to ask her name. She seems engaged and after months of therapy he's learning how to share. Dr. Staten would be proud.

"So, I've been taking stock of my life. Changing from a boy to a man. I don't drink because he did. I work out every day to release stress. I'm building a portfolio, so my finances are set. I'm friendly and fair, a good friend." He adds.

"That's nice dear to God be the Glory!" She says leaning in close to his ear when she speaks. "You seem like a nice young man." She pats him on the shoulder.

Timothy smiles at her. He's glad she cuts him off before he gets to the crux of his tirade, which involves something about "weak woman" and "bad mothers" being his only hindrance. He doubts the nice elderly woman who strokes his back and pats him on the shoulder would be as cordial if he divulges everything. *I need to get past this.* He scoots away from the woman and over a little closer to the edge of the pew to refocus his attentions to the sermon. *I have to work on my mind.*

"Your flesh needs to be on the cross and Christ needs to be on the throne! You can't become the person you really want to be or the man God calls you to be without a mind shift!" Pastor Jacob said, then the organist uses a high pitch to echo Pastor Jacob's high pitch. *Did he just say that? Did he say the word "man" out loud? I'm about to lose it* in here. He studies the sanctuary in awe to see if anyone else looks or feels as he does right now. There are people with uplifted hands, excitedly, waving them from side to side to acknowledge their agreement.

"Does anyone want prayer?" Pastor Jacob's, asks.

Some folks jump to their feet to head to the altar. He grabs the letter in his hands and clutches it in his lap. It's as if he's at the gym trying to bench more weight than he's ever benched before. He tries to push the weights up, but the force presses against him. Then, some supernatural force lightens the load of the weight and pushes his body up.

"Aren't you tired of loneliness? The never-ending battle. Looking for love or being loved too much. Don't you want to be free?" Pastor Jacobs, drills.

That was it! He must move. He can't sit in his seat any longer.

When he decides to go up for prayer, he hears the elderly woman beside him call out, "Amen."

He's not alone. Others felt it too. It's as if a great bright light shines through the church and wakes everyone up, both in their minds and hearts. They flock to the altar for prayer. Everyone except Arianna seemed to hear Pastor Jacobs' words. She sits in a daze.

He tries to get her attention but it's no use if she is in another place. Although he wants her to be a part of what's happening; he can't wait. He must apply everything he has learned in the group to this moment. Timothy has to find a way out of what's plaguing him to be free of it. As he approaches the alter, he sees Pastor Jacob rushes toward him, the pastor's hand reaches Timothy's chest before the rest of his body and Timothy's chest sinks which pushes his body three feet backwards. The power in the force of Pastor Jacob's hand hits his body causing Timothy's chest to jolt and head to burn like fire coming from a lightening bolt. With his eyes shut, his body sunken Timothy falls to knees and cries out, "I'm sorry, Lord. Please forgive me, Jesus. I need you Save, Heal and Deliver me! Thank you, God! Thank you, God!" He repeats it over and over while the tears roll off chin on to the ground. He kneels there for what seems like twenty minutes, trying to steady his whimpering and releasing all the negativity and guilt till his soul feels free. With one hand someone helps him on to his feet and gives him a couple loose tissues with the other hand. Amazingly, Timothy feels lighter. There's a pep in his step as he leaves the alter, "Is this what freedom feels like," he asks the male usher who helped him up. "Sure does...when God shows up," the usher responds with a smile.

Heading to his seat, Timothy spies out Dr. Staten in the back of the church. He smiles at her. But she doesn't notice him which is fine. In this moment, he knows he's not alone in the process.

Still, in all, after the high of the prayer fades, he realizes there's work for him to do. He shoves his mother's letter into his side pocket. "I'm mailing this letter today, then it is back to the group for me." He whispers it so the only one to hear him this time is God.

162

18

GROUP SESSION

∞"DID YOU MAIL it?" Arianna asks as Timothy positions himself comfortably in the group circle seat next to her.

"That's it!" He glares at her and scoots his seat into the small group circle. "That's all you can think to say to me? No, apologies for missing an entire month of our group sessions. Not even a how have you been?"

"Oh sorry. How have you been?" Arianna pauses. "Well, did you mail it?"

"Yes. I sent my mother the letter last week and she has already responded."

"What did she say, Timothy?" Dr. Staten appears from behind a multicolored decorative room divider.

"Oh man, I didn't even see you? I thought you were next door or in the bathroom." He says squinting his eyes.

"My parents just sent me this Peruvian wooden and glass divider as a gift."

"Is it your birthday?" He asks.

"No. It's more of a 'thinking of you' gift."

"Must be nice to have your parents love you, just because." He smirks.

"Well it's absolutely beautiful." Arianna says. "Besides, it's a nice thought."

"Yes, it is. Now back to you Timothy." Dr. Staten says. "What was your mother's response?"

"She says she's coming. We'll see if she actually shows up, though. Nonetheless, you'll be there right, Doc?" He looks at her wide eyed.

"I'm not planning to miss it." Dr. Staten smiles at him. "You know I saw you at church and your face looked thoroughly engrossed in Pastor Jacob's lesson. Why?"

"What do you mean, why?"

"What was going through your mind?"

"Everything. That woman and her husband, Melissa, or even my two sisters. Pastor makes sense when he speaks. And I was thinking I need to deal with this now. I feel better most days but then the slightest thing she does drags me to that place where I act like him."

"And what did you take away from Pastors' lesson?"

"I have to confront her and forgive them."

That's a great take away. Here's a thought, why don't you start by calling her "mother" and him "father" in place of, "that woman and her husband?"

"I don't know if I can."

"Why not try?"

"I want to. I just feel so desperate and I act desperate whenever I approach either one of them."

"You know Timothy, desperation is the womb to make bad choices. Try being less desperate and more proactive. Be open to working things out." Dr. Staten sits back in her seat and folds her hands in her lap.

"You sure are right, doc." Arianna chimes in. "I have made some awful choices out of desperation but I think I'm finally getting better. Even the weeks of my lapse in attendance. I always think of our time here and do a quick WWDSD."

"What is WWDSD, Arianna?" Timothy squints his eyes in her direction. "I bet it's something you just made up."

"No sir, well not entirely." Arianna rolls her eyes and neck at him. "It stands for What Would Dr. Staten Do, so there."

"Of course it does." Timothy nods his head. "That's not made up at all, huh." He grins.

"Thank you for thinking of me, Arianna." Dr. Staten bows affably. "However, soon you won't have to ask, what would Dr. Staten do, though?"

"I know. I'm still in the process."

"You use the word process often. I hope you're making strides in your process that move you forward. If true, stay in it till you're done. If not, push yourself." Dr. Staten says. "One thing I hope both of you gleaned from Sunday's sermon was learning to love and forgive. That's what all this boils down too. I hope you see that."

"Yes, I did. Every story theme was rooted and grounded in love." Timothy says. "I caught that."

"Me too. Although I must say there was a moment my mind went blank. I tuned out and only thoughts of Brian made its way through." Arianna admits.

"I noticed that too." He says, then, winks at her.

"Anyway." She grimaces at him. "I heard most of the sermon. I'm concerned about Brian coming out of the coma."

"Coma!" Timothy shouts. "Way to blind side us."

"Not us..." Arianna looks at Dr. Staten and back at Timothy. "She knows. She's been at the hospital practically every day with me."

"You have?"

"Yes Timothy I have. Not in the room just close enough in case she needed support."

"And you didn't share that with me?" He asks.

"It wasn't my information to share. It's Arianna's."

"I apologize Tim. I was going to tell you as soon as I saw you again." She looks at him. "Which I just did!" She says, fluttering her eyelashes at him.

"Oh yay. Thanks." Timothy says. "Although you saw me at church, too."

"True. But, it's been a lot on me. I was trying to be strong for Brian and I handle things on my own. I wanted to tell you. I didn't even allow Dr. Staten in the hospital room. Just knowing she was nearby was very helpful." Arianna looks at Dr. Staten and mouths, "Thank you."

"You're welcome." Dr. Staten scoots up in her chair closer to Arianna and Timothy. "You know you both have grown tremendously. I believe you two are stronger and more prepared for healthy confrontations than before. This is why I suggest communicating with your loved ones again. Bare all. Tell all. I believe in both of you. Love looks not with the eyes but with the mind."

"Is that another Gandhi quote?" Arianna asks.

"Not this time. It is William Shakespeare."

"You are the mistress of quotes." Arianna laughs.

Dr. Staten continues. "You choose to show love. And to quote the pastor, God is forgiveness. God is love."

"Well to quote Tina Turner, what's love got to do with it?" Arianna mocks.

"You know the answer to that, Arianna." Dr. Staten says. "You both had better know by now."

"Yes, I know. Love is everything." Arianna smiles at Dr. Staten.

"Absolutely." Dr. Staten nods.

"I hope you're right." Timothy says. "That wom-... I mean my mother will be at my exhibit. We'll see."

"Great." Says Dr. Staten.

"I'll be back at the hospital with Brian. Every day till regains consciousness." Arianna says.

"Definitely! Continue to talk to him. Read to him. Tell him all your secrets as a dress rehearsal for when he comes out of the coma. I can also keep up his brain activity"

"Thank you for saying *when* and not *if,* doc." Arianna says.

Timothy taps Arianna on the shoulder. "Hey, I believe he's coming out of the coma too."

"Honestly you do?"

"Without question. If you can sit in a hospital room day after day, knowing what I know about your past, I can surely confront my mother. A peaceful confrontation. I can be as strong as you."

"You think I'm strong?" Arianna asks.

"Yes, I truly do." Timothy says.

"Both of you can. Timothy, I believe it." Dr. Staten encourages him.

He gets up from his seat, grabs his things and walks toward the door. "You know this was a good group session today. I have to put the final touches on my pieces." He calls, "Later doc. Later Arianna."

"Good bye Timothy." They call back in unison.

19

Is every Hospital a DEJA VU

∞**THE PAVEMENT BENEATH** my feet are gravelly and uneven as I run down my driveway and struggle up the incline from my house to the corner. When I reach the first corner I stop to bend over, pressing my hands against the crevice of my upper thigh to catch my breath.

Run, run as fast as you can. You can't catch me, I'm alone again.
Run, run as fast as you can. You can't catch me, I'm alone again.

Each time my feet hit the pavement in a rhythmic beat like a drum, I wonder what Brian's doing at the moment rather than continue to chant.

He's somewhere in the place where he's not completely here or completely gone either. I need him to come back to me.

Run, run as fast as you can. You can't catch me, I'm alone again.

Steadily, I continue to charge up the steep hill, pumping my arms back-and-forth as they push against the wind. I run. Then, I run faster. I run away from my house leading my body deeper into the neighborhood. Pushing the thoughts as far out of my mind as the distance that separates me from my home. The goal is to leave a grave distance from everything and everyone. I even get up earlier than usual, so I don't have to fear any intrusion from my couple-jogging neighbors.

I run through the neighborhood studying lavish homes, tree-lined streets, SLOW DOWN and CHILDREN AT PLAY signs, but no stop lights. Nothing tells me to halt, so I push on. Eventually, I'll have to stop running to gauge the distance I've run but I've been doing a good job of keeping my mind preoccupied and clear of thoughts of him.

At least for the moment, then, I wonder when he'll open his eyes from the coma. He has to come back to me. I push myself again, pumping my arms to gain momentum. I have to do something-anything to forget. *Think about work, Arianna.* I try to picture the unsold properties in my listing. Making a mental note of all follow up calls and scheduling, I still have yet to do.

"The beautiful colonial on North Union in Cranford should sell soon. That million dollar listing should put me over the top and secure my realtor of the year award." I say it breathlessly jogging through the neighborhood.

By the time I notice how far I've run, I realize I'm in a different town. The homes a little less lavish still pleasant enough for me to feel safe jogging. It's a place I've never been. Where am I? Literally, and Metaphorically. I try to read the street signs quickly as I pass, my feet don't stop. They keep moving. *Jefferson, Roosevelt, Kennedy, it's like a game. Why do they seem familiar? Now I see Madison, Wilson, and Washington. Oh... I got it! They are the names of dead presidents. Oh no... dead people.*

Run, run as fast as you can. You can't catch me, I'm alone again.

Am I lost in this metaphor? No. Technically I am only one town over. I know how to get home from here.

Two hours and 5 miles later I can feel the finish line approaching. I only have to head down this last hill, and a few feet to my driveway. "If I can find my way back then why is it too difficult for Brian?" I say it out loud.

"Good morning Ariana!" One of my couple jogging neighbors, the Benderville's, called to me and waved. I thought I could escape them, but before I could get to my house they found me.

"Morning Mr. and Mrs. Benderville!" I call back with a huge smile.

"Lovely day for a walk, huh? I'm glad it is finally warm enough to get out of the house and move." Mrs. Benderville calls to me, her husband smiling and nodding at her every word.

"Yes it is." I say giving her a quick thumbs up. It hurts to pretend, so I dart up my driveway before they can continue the conversation.

When I arrive at the hospital, I sit by Brian's side, gently taking his hand in a mine and pray.

Dear God,

Please let him live. I can't go through another loss. This is me, Arianna, confronting my problems and asking that YOUR love prevail. I'll open up to him. I'll let him in and won't have to cut myself anymore. I'll talk about my parents. He's all I have. The one I want. He's who I need. Whatever the ailment, help him- merciful God. Please.

I pull the letter out of my pocket to read to him, to tell him about my need to be a fixer, which is why not fixing him is draining me.

Every day there's a new story to tell him as interesting as Dr. Staten's group session and my confession of cutting and Timothy's admission to battering women. I even tell him about Pastor Jacobs' sermon and the entranced Timothy is engrossed in the sermon. I ramble on. Moreover, how my mind is too consumed by thoughts of him to focus, as I ought to; as well as mentioning Aunt Maria and Uncle Edward who live in Cranford, whom I'd love him to meet, the moment he wakes up!

I hold onto Brian at every visit, habitually praying for him. Somehow, the prayers roll off my lips, and in a whisper, into his ears.

Brian remains unconscious, but I feel there's a difference in him, which may be entirely in my mind. Still, I am encouraged. He's the priority. I will not abscond. I feel strength in me that's more powerful than a blade.

The nurse knows me by name now. She calls me Ms. Arianna which helps her keep our conversations professional without making me feel like an old woman, by calling me Ms. Dickerson. When Dr. Bussy and I are in the room together, he shares a new explanation regarding Brian's conditions. Mainly, the blunt force of the head trauma, messes up how Brian's brain cells work; which is what causes

173

the coma. I don't understand all the terminology he uses, nonetheless I extrapolate keywords to simplify it.

He encourages me, when he says, "He's alive. It's just that his brain is functioning at its lowest stage of alertness. We'll just have to wait and see."

"Alright. Thank you doctor." I say.

∞∞∞∞

I sit by his bed fourteen days and nights until one Monday afternoon when Brian opens his eyes, slowly scanning the room. His eyes finally land on me and stop. He squints at me as if I'm a distant memory of someone forgotten. I can tell his soul is searching for me so, I smile.

"It's me Arianna, don't try to talk." I say. "Nurse!" I ran out of the room in pursuit of someone qualified to help.

When I return with the doctor, Brian looks at me and I smile. I know he's groggy, so I am still strange to him. But, all I can think is He's alive!

It takes him a few days before he returns to normal and fully functional, like before. I'm in awe that he can recollect anything.

"I remember hearing your voice reading to me."

"You did."

"Yes but it's just your voice, no words."

"What about the accident?"

"Oh yeah, the accident. The rain was coming down really hard and I was listening to a song on my XM radio station. It was a love song that reminded me of you and I drove faster. I swerved too hard on a curve and the car hydroplaned off the road. I was going over the side. The last thing I remember thinking before everything went black and my car heading toward a tree is the thought of you waiting for me at the restaurant, alone."

"I was the last thought on your mind?"

"Yep. Then....kaboom....it was me against nature and nature won." He says rubbing his head.

"Oh boy. I'm sorry, Bri."

"Don't do that to yourself. It's not your fault." He says.

We use his recovery time and extra days' stay at the hospital to repeat the sentiments I shared when he was unconscious and talk. I begin with my parent's and how it led to me cutting myself.

"Why didn't you tell me this before?"

"I was afraid."

"Of what, Arianna?"

"Of you not loving me because of all my damage. Or worse, you leaving me."

"I have been waiting for you, begging you to even talk to me. I'm not the kind who leaves." He says.

"Please," I grab his hand "Don't strain yourself. This is supposed to be a slow recovery process. I don't want you to overdo it."

"There you go again." Brian sits up in the bed. "I'm not made of glass. I'm tougher than you think. And I can be here for you."

"Are you sure?"

"Yes."

"Will you tell me if it gets to be too much for you?" I pause. "You know, and you want to leave?"

"I won't."

"Brian you don't know that."

"I know me."

"Patronize me, okay. Agree you'll tell me if it becomes too much."

"Fo'sho beautiful."

I smile at him and for the first time I feel weightless. I can breathe. "Well how much do you want to know?"

"How much is there?"

"A lot."

"Well, I better get comfortable." He leans up "Can you prop up the pillows under me so I can relax?" He smiles, and I see my old friends, dimple left and dimple right.

"You want to do this here?" I say squishing pillows behind his back. "It can wait till you're out of here and back home."

"No more waiting, Arianna. I have nothing but time."

"I guess I should start with I love you." The words come out easier than I'd imagine.

"Back'atcha beautiful." He reaches for my hand. "I love you too." He says.

I breathe in gently; then, smile into my exhale.

20

OH, TIMOTHY!

∞*SHE SAID YES*. Timothy walks into his oversized bedroom closet to get his black Hugo Boss tux, crisp white shirt, gold and black cufflinks and his gold pinstripe tie from the Boss collection to finish the look for the black-tie affair. He grabs the black polish and brushes to give his alligator skin shoes the once over to make sure they pop. She said yes, she'll be there, alone. He repeats to himself.

He knows he should be concentrating on the exhibit but the knots in his stomach and racing heartbeat beat are pure adrenaline, over her. The past year has been leading up to this moment or at least that's what it feels like. His work with Dr. Staten, even before the group sessions, points him toward this moment. *What if this time is no better than last time? What if we end up arguing in front of all my guests?* Thoughts of "what if's" occupy him; still, he's willing to do whatever it takes to make the evening go well.

He's been practicing using the word "mother" not "Priscilla" or "woman" when speaking with her. He'll start with small talk to engage her, as often as possible, while also making himself accessible to the hundreds of other guests who frequent his exhibits. And if she's a no show, no harm - no foul, because he had to attend regardless, it's his gallery showing the exhibit. Plus, Dr. Staten will definitely be there, she never disappoints, which is incentive for him to invite his mother.

Dr. Staten will be there for moral support.

Timothy races around his room pacing from one corner to the other. He goes into the bathroom to shower, shave and do a little-last minute grooming before walking out the door and hopping into the limo waiting to chauffeur him to Princeton University.

By the time he arrives, droves of guests are in the gallery hoarding over his collection. Dr. Staten mingles with a group of people he's

179

seen at other exhibits. She makes acquaintances easily. Timothy notices his mother, when she enters and heads to the back of the room. She browses through the exhibit studying the mounted painting, metal sculptors and clay models symmetrically scattered throughout the room. When she looks at him, he holds her gaze, while continuing his conversation with a frequenter. He smiles at her as she walks toward him.

"Excuse me." She says politely. "Is the entire exhibit of your work?"

"Yes, it is." Timothy pats the man on the shoulder. "This is my old friend, Professor Dominique Ledreaux. He's an Art Professor from a University in France." He points at his mother, "Professeur, c'est ma mère, Madame Priscilla Foxx."

"Tim, I had no idea you spoke French." His mother says.

"A little." He says.

"Bonjour." Professor Ledreaux smiles gently and bows his head. "I never miss one of your son's exhibits. He has such a powerful voice in his work. You agree, no?" He laughs.

"Oh my, you speak English." She shakes her head at Timothy. "Yes he is quite talented."

"Thank you both. Professor Ledreaux, please excuse us. I want to show my mother the crux of my collection."

"Of course. There is much to see. We can catch up later. Oui?"

"Oui."

"Au revoir." Professor Ledreaux nods at Timothy, smiles at his mother then heads toward the "stills" at the opposite side of the gallery.

"I'm glad you were able to make it, Mother."

"I am proud of the work you're doing, Timothy. Also, extremely humbled by the invitation."

"Here," he directs her to a painting leaning against a display in the middle of the room. There are two bright flood lights hanging above the corners of the painting so the images and colors illuminate from the canvass. The painting is of a faceless woman who hangs her head, drained. In, place of her heart, is a big black space. She has five arms, one holds a child, another covers her face, a third balances the world like a weight, a fourth grasps the heart of a man lying next to her, and a fifth hand stirs a pot of stew. Aside from the cinnamon tone in her neck, hands, legs, and colors in her dress, the core of her is devoid of color, simply blackness. "This is the heart of my collection."

Timothy watched his mother stare at the painting intently. A tear slides down the side of her cheek. Which she doesn't brush away, then another. She simply lets them roll down her cheek slow and steady until they fall off her chin and onto the collar of her dress. Her eyes never leave the painting.

"Are you alright?" He asks. "Do you like it?"

Now, one tear has turned into many tears. She's crying but it doesn't seem like a sorrowful cry to him. "I never realized how famous you were in the art world. You have such talent and belief in your work. Also, people come from all directions to admire your exhibition? Amazing turnout, dear."

Timothy is quiet.

He sees her in a new light, for the first time.

"You know I spied this painting the moment I walked into the room. I was drawn to it. I was actually heading over here, to study it more thoroughly, then I saw you looking at me." His mother says. The detail of the woman in the painting is mesmerizing.

Then, Professor Ledreaux beckons Timothy to come over with a quick wave of his hand. He's standing in front of a clay sculpture of a lion, with a group of people who whisper to one another as they stoke the curvature of the crown and the mass of its legs.

"Mother, I apologize but I am being summoned by Professor Ledreux and some other guests." He touches her shoulder. "I'll be back, directly. Please, walk around to see the rest of the exhibit. We'll reconnect afterward for a cup of coffee, okay? How does that sound?"

"Perfect dear. Go on. Don't worry about me." She says.

From across the room, Timothy notices his mother, still gazing at the painting. She hasn't moved an inch. Other guests are walking around, remarking, commenting on their favorite pieces, trying to decipher the intent and meaning of each art piece. But not his mother. The painting of the woman is intriguing to her. Timothy watches her.

He walks through swarms of smiling faces, groping his clothes or attempting to shake his hand, toward his mother. She doesn't notice his approach, that doesn't bother him. It's the breeze that comes through the door when it opens that jolts her concentration. She shivers enough to realize she is not alone and has an audience. Timothy is standing behind her.

"When did you get back?" She asks without turning to face him. He's silent.

"What do you call her?"

It always amazes him how intelligent his mother is, how quickly she understands his artistry, the ability to identify the painting as "her" recognizing it's a life force and not only colors on a page. He often thought someone who would put up with an uneducated, pseudo-Cherokee, alcoholic would have to be equally uneducated, that is not his mother. She is an outstanding Master's degree-holding educator. This is why he could never deal with her settling for a man like Yancy.

"The Soul-less Woman." He responds.

"Why would you give beauty such a name?"

"I was going to call her the Faceless Mother but as I got to know this person, I realized she is more than a mother; she is a woman. Although she holds many things which should bring her happiness, she is missing a vital piece, her soul." He replies.

"Oh, I see." She starts to cry. Priscilla quickly wipes the tears away. But the tears keep flowing as if a stream flowing down a rock. The painting had an undeniable effect on his mother.

"Do you like it?"

"Yes, very much dear," she smiles at him. Then returns to the painting.

Her reaction is unexpected. His initial thoughts were she'd be angry, defensive or in disbelief that he could paint something so dark. Tearful and purging never crosses his mind.

"The exhibit is about to end. Would you like to come with me to the café across the street?" He asks.

"Yes. I'll stay here until you're ready to go."

"Wouldn't you like to see the rest of the exhibit?" He asks.

"No dear. I see all of your worth through this masterpiece." She points at the painting. "Timothy, you are worth millions!" She turns toward him, kisses him on the cheek, then, she returns her focus on the painting.

He touches his cheek where her lips met his face and smiles. When he skims the crowded room in search of his next stop in his final round as host, he notices Dr. Staten smiling at him.

"Hello there." He says as he approaches her, "have you been here the whole time?"

"Yes. I told you I wasn't planning to miss it. Is that your mother over there?" She points to the woman standing in front of a display in the center of the room.

"Yes. We are about to go grab a cup of coffee at the cafe and talk."

"Excellent. I'm getting ready to head out but couldn't leave without saying how marvelous your exhibit is. You are a talented man and there's such a powerful voice through your work."

"Thank you."

"See you next week for our final session?" She leans in to ask him privately.

"I'll be there." He whispers back and laughs. "Later doc."

+ + +

At the café, Timothy, and his mother talk earnestly. In between the sips of her hot Chai tea, and his tall Cappuccino, they share pieces of their life. Priscilla explains the challenges in her marriage and her inbred need to be selfless for her children, anything, to keep her family together.

"I was raised to believe, families should stay together. You weather the storm as a unit- husband, wife and children. The father was the captain. The wife as the anchor steading the ship called life, as we sail." She lowers her eyes and cups her tea with both hands as she lifts it to her mouth. "When you have such learned behavior as a child, it's immensely difficult to react differently. My mother would say that marriage is forever and you do whatever is needed to keep your family together."

"But we were never together. He was too abusive to be the captain." Timothy is cautious of his tone. "You anchored us indeed. We were stuck in the same spot for years."

"Yes you're right. I see that now. Back then it wasn't as clear. How will we make it on our own, is all I could think about. Especially with Yancy being the sole provider. In the beginning, we agreed he'd work while I got my Masters." Timothy's forehead wrinkles up when he squints at her. "Yes, your father worked and watched you all; while I finished school."

"I don't remember him staying home."

"I know you were a baby. He held our house together, then. I was in school every day- all day working on an accelerated Masters' Degree program. He wasn't always an abusive drunk, as you call him." She caresses the rim of the cup at the thought of it. "Prior to drinking, he was a loving husband. You know what he would say to me?"

Timothy shakes his head no.

"He'd say, I love you more than I've loved anything in my life. It's hard to leave after that. Instead, I kept hoping and praying, one day the person who spoke of his love toward me in such a powerful way would return." She smiles at Timothy. "It wasn't all bad."

"I don't remember that part."

"I know."

"I mean, I never got the chance to know that side of him. All I remember is the heavy handed, harsh toned drunk. I grew up in that reality. It's difficult to see him any other way."

"I understand and for that I am sorry. The two of you are so similar."

"You know, I didn't inherit his drinking; just the abuse toward women." Timothy places one hand over his mother's hands as she grips her cup. "I'm not proud of it. That's why I'm getting counseling. I want to be a gentle, loving man and not lash out at women in anger. Every day, I'm learning how to resolve conflict, a different way."

"Yes, I can tell the therapy is working. The last time you were home, during the argument with your father, you walked away, instead of striking back; I could see the difference in you."

"You could?"

"Yes. This made me realize that I need to ask for help. When I realized that there was no change in Yancy, I found a therapist, and he did not try to make any permanent changes. He must walk this path of recovery alone. I can't enable him any longer. That's why I asked him to move out, while I focus on my emotional health."

Timothy's eyes widened. "Honestly?"

"Yes he's been staying with a friend. I heard he was attending AA meetings."

He looks at her.

"His friend Frederick, calls me and gives me updates. I doubt Yancy even knows we've been conversing."

"Are you alright living on your own?" He asks.

"Yes. It's honestly because of you. During the treatment, I became stronger every day. I talk to your sisters every week. They all know that your father moved out. Most days, they call me to encourage me."

Timothy is wide-eyed, and his mouth drops open. *Unbelievable. She left his father and it's attributed to me?* "I don't know what to say."

"There's nothing for you to say, dear. I want you to know that your Father and I are going to be alright. Whether we end up together or remain apart. We are trying to do better by ourselves and you."

He looks down to see both his cup, and his mother's cup, empty. There are two half-eaten bran muffins and a slice of pecan pie on the plate in the center of the table. "Would you like a refill?" He pointed to her cup. "Or some real food instead of these dessert snacks? My treat."

"No dear. I really must go." She rises off the chair. "It has been an honor." She leans down and kisses the top of his head. "You are a brilliant man."

He doesn't squirm at the touch of her lips and there is no awkward feeling in the pit of his stomach. "Thank you." He pauses. "Mother."

She smiles at him when he calls her mother. "I love you."

He lets the four letter word roll off her tongue, through his ear gate and straight to his heart. A warm feeling grips him. "Goodbye Mother." He says as he stands to give her a hug. Although he isn't ready to say, "I love you back," at this moment, he understands and forgives her. The rest will come in time.

Timothy sits in the cafe at the table alone, as his mother walks out the door. He pulls his cell phone out of his pocket and dials a number. This time, he doesn't struggle with letting the call go through. He knows what he wants to say, and with whom he needs to speak. There are three short beeps before the voicemail is clicked. He can tell by how quickly the message begins, the woman on the other end, sees his number and decides to send him straight to voicemail. So, he decides to leave a message:

Hello, there. I understand why you're upset and don't blame you for not wanting to answer my call. I've done many unspeakably cruel things to you. But, I'm working hard to change into a better man. Anyhow, I only called to say, I apologize for all my physical and emotional cruelty toward you. I am truly sorry, Melissa.

When Timothy finished his last sentence, the tape recorder beeped. He hung up the phone and put it on the table.

21

GROUP SESSION

∞**WHEN TIMOTHY AND** Arianna arrive at the group, the circle of chairs is larger than usual; instead of the intimate setting of three chairs there are six chairs randomly placed in a make-shift way. Timothy searches for Dr. Staten's and Arianna's familiar faces and smiles. Arianna takes the seat on his left as usual and Dr. Staten is on his right. The other three newcomers sit across from him.

"Hello there." Dr. Stanten says. "For a couple of you this is your first time in a group setting. For my regular group participants, these are your last group meetings, and your level of growth is shocking. So much so, I thought it befitting for you to speak with the newcomers. If that's alright and you are willing to share?"

"Fine with me." Arianna says first.

"What would you like us to share?" Timothy asks.

"Well first why don't we go around the room and do a quick introduction. Then we'll come back to your question." Dr. Staten suggests.

"Hey there everyone I'm Arianna." She gave a short wave.

"Hello I am Timothy." He bows his head courteously.

"I'm Christopher." The tall and thin black-haired man said suddenly.

"Hi everyone my name is Storie." The pale skinned woman with dirty blonde hair and hazel eyes says, then smiles. She looks over at Timothy who keeps his gaze on her longer than usual. She smiles at him and bats her eyelashes.

"I guess that just leaves me. I am Michael Louis Murphy." He prowls the group like a lion in search of a lioness and smiles when his eyes connect with Ariana's.

Arianna smiles back at him. I have Brian. I have Brian. She repeats inwardly.

"Great and as you all know, I am Dr. Staten." She turned to Timothy and Arianna. "Why don't you each briefly share one thing you've learned in a group that has helped you?"

Timothy looks at Arianna, "Ladies first."

"Well I guess I'm up first." She grits her teeth at Timothy.

"Ooh a biter... nice." Michael says seductively.

Arianna looks at Timothy and laughs, "No an ex-cutter." She winks at Michael. "I guess one of the major things I've learned is how to give and receive love. I've lived with secrets, keeping everything in, trying to hoard my love. But it made me weak, sad and desperate. When people are desperate, they will do incredible things. Not anymore."

"Thank you Arianna," says Dr. Staten. "Timothy, and you."

"Forgiveness is my takeaway. Perhaps not how you may think, though. I've done some unspeakable things in anger. I've learned how to forgive myself which is the hardest part, so confronting my demons gets easier day by day. Now I can forgive others."

"Well, I could not have said it better. Love and forgiveness are what we work toward in our group. We reach the most intimate parts of ourselves to move through our struggles. When we say the word intimacy, we're saying "in to me see"- what has been is no more, but what shall be is now." Dr. Staten's gaze bounces from one person to the next.

Arianna nods her head in agreement.

Timothy searches the group trying to decipher who will make it to the other side unscathed and who will quit. I didn't quit. However, both he and Arianna leaped huge hurdles, continuing to live their lives in a healthy way. He worked daily on his relationship with his mother and perhaps with his father, as well. Arianna's relationship with Brian might end tomorrow or span the space of decades- who knows? Deep down, he knows, they'll both survive.

Finally, the last person he noticed was Storie. Her petite frame, high boned structured face and friendly demeanor is intoxicating. He looks at her and is intuitively drawn in. Maybe, it's the fact that there's a real underlying story locked away in her. "No that's not it. She reminds me of my mother," he whispers. Timothy phone buzzes. He grabs it from his pocket and sees he has a missed call from Melissa.

Made in the USA
Middletown, DE
25 March 2023

27241366R00106